I0663569

SNOWED

Boston Rebels, book 3

RJ SCOTT

V.L. LOCEY

Love Lane Books

Copyright

Snowed (Boston Rebels #3)

Copyright © 2021 RJ Scott, Copyright © 2021 V.L. Locey

Cover design by Meredith Russell, Edited by Kathy Krick

Published by Love Lane Books Limited

ISBN - 9781785645884

All Rights Reserved

This literary work may not be reproduced or transmitted in any form or by any means, including electronic or photographic reproduction, in whole or in part, without express written permission. This book cannot be copied in any format, sold, or otherwise transferred from your computer to another through upload to a file sharing peer-to-peer program, for free or for a fee. Such action is illegal and in violation of Copyright Law.

All characters and events in this book are fictitious. Any resemblance to actual persons living or dead is strictly coincidental.

All trademarks are the property of their respective owners.

Snowed (Boston Rebels, 3)

A second chance at love is all Kyle wants for Christmas, but a dark menace from his past wants him dead, and love is second to staying alive.

Kyle Lourenco has carved out a comfortable life and career for himself in Boston. With the holidays quickly approaching, he's heading home for the first time in several years. Home to his loving parents and the small Canadian town where he was raised. And home to Christian, his best friend and the first man to steal his heart.

Just as a winter storm begins to blow in, it forces Kyle off the road only miles from home and a dark and sinister force from his past creeps ever closer. His only hope is getting to Christian's cabin before the evil that has haunted him for years finally catches up to him.

Best friends since they were three, Christian Gauthier grew up next door to Kyle, in a remote mountain town with one stoplight and a forty-mile round trip to the nearest school. When Kyle left town for a shot at a professional hockey career, he took Christian's heart with him. Even though he knew Kyle was always destined for bigger things, it hadn't stopped Christian from falling for him as soon as he knew what love was.

With Christmas coming soon and a major snowstorm heading their way, Christian shuts the doors to the family store and heads to his cabin, where he will be on standby as an official volunteer for Search and Rescue. He has never regretted staying in Eagle Ridge, but a near miss on a simple rescue leads him to reevaluate everything, and when Kyle ends up at his door, he knows that guarding his heart might not be the best solution after all.

Dedication

To my family who accepts me and all my foibles and quirks. Even the plastic banana in my holster.
VL Locey

Always for my family.
RJ Scott

SNOWED

BOSTON REBELS BOOK 3

RJ SCOTT & V.L. LOCEY

Love Lane Books

ONE

Kyle

THE FLURRY OF ACTION IN THE CORNER HAD MY attention.

Our captain was locked up with Alex Garcia, one of the young stallions on the Arizona Raptors' roster. The puck was under Alex's skate by the looks. To be honest, it was kind of hard to tell from my position in net, as more Rebels and Raptors joined the knot.

I glanced back when a shout nearby erupted. Apparently, Austin Rowe had said something that had an incredibly bad impact on the Raptors captain, Vladislav Novikov, the massive Russian who looked like Dolph Lundgren in *Rocky IV* and was nicknamed "Iceberg" due to his icy personality. Vlad looked furious, which was rather scary.

It was unusual for Austin to say *anything* that would ever make anyone mad. My roommate was one of the sweetest guys I had ever met. Well, Austin might be second to Christian Gauthier from back home in Eagle Ridge, Manitoba. Thinking of Christian was too distracting, so I shook away the bittersweet images of times past and glanced to the corner.

One of the linesmen had started shouting at the players to break it up and get the puck into play. Something—or someone—impacted me hard. As I went down in a tangle with Vlad on top of me, my shoulder popped out of the socket. The pain was incredible. My left arm went completely numb after a few seconds. My net popped off its moorings. A rush of shapes—my teammates, I was sure —moved around me as I lay on the ice moaning in pain.

"Sorry, he pushed me," Vlad said as he was pulled off me by Marquis, then slapped upside his head. Vlad, being a hockey player, slapped Marquis back. Tate Collins got into the scrum, but not to throw punches. He was on one knee beside me, protecting me from the snarl of players now throwing down gloves.

"You hurt?" Tate asked as I was finally freed from the massive Russian. I growled out a reply, then rolled from my injured shoulder to my good one. Jaw locked, fighting back tears, I cursed madly, knowing this was far more than a dislocated shoulder. I'd felt something rip. "Lie still," Tate said, his hand on my hip as he turned to bellow for our trainer. "It's okay, man, you're good. Here's your captain."

"Renco, hey, Wally's coming," Xander said, trying to get me to my skates. I nodded, gritted my teeth, and cradled my left arm in my right hand. Blinking away the dampness, I saw our new backup goalie getting on his gear. Generally, I would have fought to stay in, but there was no way I was going to finish this game. That sucked. We only played the Raptors twice a year, and the next time would be in late April out in Arizona. I'd really wanted a win against this team that had clawed its way out of the NHL sewers to be a true contender for the Cup. Wally arrived, his face a mask of concern, and started peppering me with questions.

"It's bad," I ground out and that was it. I was helped to my skates and then off the ice, Wally and Xander at my side, as the Rebels fans clapped and both teams tapped their sticks on the ice.

"It'll be fine, Renco," Xander said before I stepped off the ice, my vision blurring at the white-hot pain in my shoulder. I appreciated his cheery words, but knew, deep down, it was going to be anything but fine.

———

IT TOOK A LITTLE OVER TWO HOURS FOR THE SURGEONS AT the hospital to verify what I already knew. I'd torn something in my rotator cuff upon impact with Vlad, who, as it turned out, had been shoved into me by Austin. I'd watched the replay a dozen times as I'd been poked, prodded, x-rayed, and flirted with by a really cute nurse named Tim. Not that I was interested in Tim or any other guy right now. I was in too much pain and feeling as low as a seal's belly, as Pop would say. Ugh. I'd have to call my parents when I got home and tell them the bad news. Both had been watching the game—they never missed one. Mom had already called as I'd been riding to the hospital in the back of an ambulance. Nick had insisted on the ambulance, and who was I to argue with the team owner?

The tear would require arthroscopic surgery and would put me on the injured reserve list for one to six months. My eyeballs nearly fell out of my head when the chief of sports medicine said that. I doubted it would be six months. I'd work hard, do therapy several times a week, and be back in net by the end of the All-Star break. At least I didn't have to worry about a place on the Olympic team representing Canada, because DiCosta and Delaney had those main spots, each the best kind of goalies in their own right.

My heart hadn't been in it because I wasn't even disappointed.

I sighed, wincing at the dull throb in my shoulder, and watched the replay of the end of the game on my phone as a nurse—not cute Tim—fiddled with the IV in my right arm. They were giving me some pain meds, which was nice. I was scheduled for surgery tomorrow at six a.m. and would be sent home a day or two later. The nurse humming "Jingle Bells" as she moved around the room taking vitals and plumping pillows.

"You have some company waiting in the hall." I looked up from my phone. She was an older woman with graying hair and a kind smile. Her name tag said "Mona."

My head was getting a little sloppy as the pain meds kicked in.

"Is it my parents?" I asked, then corrected myself. "No, I know it's not them. They're in Eagle Ridge. That's in Manitoba. Right on Hudson Bay. Pops says we have more polar bears than people in Eagle Ridge."

She gave me a smile. "I'd stay away from the polar bears, if I were you."

"Oh yah, we do."

"Visiting hours are over, but Dr. Kalmar said they could come for a few minutes." She offered me some water, which I declined, as the creeping dread I carried deep in my psyche flared up.

"Who is it?" I asked, clutching my phone in my hand as a wave of something near panic bubbled to the surface. My heart rate started to spike. Not even the meds that made things soft could keep away the sudden fear that gripped me—that someone was out there wanting to hurt me. The fears that I always carried with me, and the shadows I jumped at, were right next to me as Mona gave me a worried look.

"Your teammates. Shall I send them home?"

Relief flooded me. No one was here to hurt me. No one was waiting for a moment to drag me from my bed and kill me. I was safe.

I'm safe.

"No, no, please send them in." The unexplained anxiety quieted a bit, knowing that someone would be in the room with me. She gave me a long look. "I'm good.

Just feeling a little funny from the medication. I'd like to see them."

She gave me a maternal look that made me pine for my mother. "Five minutes, no more."

I worked up a smile. "Thank you. Five minutes." She left, and I melted back into the too-stiff pillows behind me. Eyes closed, I took a cleansing breath. It was fine. All was fine. There was nothing here to hurt me. The hospital was safe. Filled with people. The shadow man couldn't get me in here. I was fine. Safe. I was safe.

"Hey," Xander's soft voice pulled me from the abyss of mysterious, unnamable fear that rode my back. "Nurse Mona said we had five minutes."

I saw Austin slip in behind Xander with a hangdog look, his bright eyes melancholy.

"I'm having surgery tomorrow," I said for no sensible reason. "I have a sling." I tried to lift my arm and was rewarded with a zing of pain that raced to my toes. "I have medication too."

"Yeah, we can see." Xander nudged Austin forward as he smiled at me. I liked Xander. He was gay, like me, and was a good captain. Just as good as Brady Rowe, Austin's cousin, had been. "Austin wanted to talk to you badly. I told him you needed rest, but he insisted."

"Okay." I felt sluggish and silly, the creeping unseen that prowled my nightmares pushed back into the shadows by the arrival of my friends. This was why I always had a roommate. The unseen only came at me in the darkest, loneliest places like sleep.

"I'm super sorry," Austin stated, standing beside my bed, looking blue. "I was trying to get under Novikov's skin, you know, like Marquis and Moral do, right? But when I try to chirp people, they either snort at me as if I were stupid or they get mad. Vlad got mad. He called me a stupid baby who could never hope to be as talented at Tennant and should stick to sharpening Ten's skates."

"Ouch," I said, and not because my shoulder hurt.

Austin sighed. Xander patted his shoulder.

"I lost my temper and shoved him. Right into you," Austin whispered as he stared down at his sneakers.

"It happens. Accidents. It's slippery on the ice," I replied, hoping I didn't sound as fuzzy as I was feeling. Austin's bright eyes lifted from the floor. "It's good yeah. I get to go home for the holidays. It's been years. Pops and Mom will make food for days. Did you know that polar bears can smell their prey up to a kilometer away?"

"We didn't know that. Cool trivia!" Xander said as Austin gaped at me. "So, now that Rowe has apologized for being a bonehead and you're not mad at him, we're going home. We'll drop by tomorrow after your surgery, okay?"

"I bet Mom makes flapper pie," I replied. They both smiled, then kind of melted away as I slipped into a deep and thankfully dream-free sleep.

I DID A LOT OF SLEEPING FOR A DAY OR SO AFTER THE surgery. All of it at home and with Austin there most of the time. He still felt bad and was fetching me everything I asked for, as well as things I didn't ask for. He heated me soup, changed my socks, made me tea, and tried to comb my hair. When he offered to help me use the toilet, I drew the line. Politely of course because I am Canadian, and Austin is a nice guy. We watched old movies—lots of *Rocky,* as I loved Sly Stallone flicks—and wrapped presents. Austin wrapped. I sat there in my pajamas with my arm in a sling being utterly useless and grumpy. Austin claimed I was far from grumpy, but I felt grumpy. Like a polar bear with a burr on its butt. I was beginning to notice that people from Eagle Ridge have a lot of polar bear references.

When Austin wasn't home, I pulled my old wooden goalie paddle out from under the bed and tucked it under the covers. No one knew I did that, thank God. It was a childhood thing, a way of calming myself when the unseen would appear at night or in my dreams. It was stupid for a twenty-five-year-old man to sleep with a kid's hockey stick... I knew that. My life would be better if I slept with men. A man. Christian. The only man I'd ever slept with, if I were being honest. Not that I hadn't had chances to have sex with guys. I did, lots of them, but they weren't quite what I was looking for in a man. They weren't Christian.

For a long time, I wondered if there was something off with me and my libido. I wanted sex. I enjoyed sex, I even yearned for it at times, but when the opportunity presented itself, I would balk. As when I'd been in Aruba with the guys for Xander's thirtieth birthday. One of the hotel bellhops had come onto me big time, making it really clear he would bring me whatever I wanted. He was cute in a blond twink sort of way, and no one would have known.

Being gay wasn't the issue. It was me. After a long time spent reading and dwelling on my sexuality, I came to the conclusion that I was gay *and* demiromantic. Having casual sex just didn't do it for me. I had to have a romantic connection first. And since I traveled all the time, and was on the ice when I wasn't in the air, that left little time for romance. Seeing as how I had to have that connection to a person before I could sleep with them...

Yeah. I spent a lot of time jerking off while fantasizing about the way Christian kissed or the way he would call my name in a heated rush as he came.

But Christian was a thing from the past, and he'd moved on when I'd moved away. He was in Manitoba 'being fabulous' according to my parents. Working in the Gauthier family store, part-timing as a search and rescue volunteer, and coaching the Eagle Ridge Eaglets junior hockey team. And here I was in Boston, playing on an NHL team and being... well, not fabulous.

"Do you want help packing?" Austin asked as I lugged a suitcase out of my closet, then tossed it to my bed. He was hovering, being sweet and solicitous, as I bumbled around with my arm in a sling.

"No thanks. I can do it." I gave him a forced smile. It

felt odd to be getting ready to go home with presents in red and green wrapping paper to take to my parents. Generally, it was the summer whenever I managed short trips home but I mostly stayed in Boston and invited my parents visit me. I cited my need to be here as business. Which was partly true. I did own half of a whale watching/deep-sea fishing charter business that operated out of the harbor. So, I spent a lot of time on the sea, which was something I'd grown to love as a kid being raised beside Hudson Bay. But a lot of my reticence about going home was because Christian was there. I think Mom suspected that, but she never said it. "I'm going to miss traveling with you guys."

"I'm sorry," Austin whispered. I knew he was.

"It's okay. Really, I needed to go home and recharge." That was a lie. I did *not* need to go back to Manitoba and see Christian. "This will be a nice break! I'll do my rehab at home, eat lots of great food, and come back in time for the playoff run."

He tried to smile, but failed. "Yeah, sure. Let me carry that to the curb when you're ready to go, okay?"

"I'm not leaving for another two days," I reminded him. Two days. *Shit.* Maybe I should actually tell my parents I was coming home. My last call with them was all about rehab and how Christmas would be quiet, but there was something in Mom's tone, a deep sadness that slapped me around the face and told me I needed to man the fuck up and get my weary ass home—if only for a few days. Best-case scenario I would roll up to their house and surprise them, see their excited faces, and we would have the best Christmas ever—I could even see Christian. But my alternative best-case scenario was that something would happen to keep me in Boston, and maybe I paid for them to come here instead. *Maybe I should do that? Then I wouldn't have to see Christian at all. Or Eagle Ridge. Or the resignation in my parents' eyes because I hardly ever went home.*

"Yeah, I know," Austin continued and yanked me out of my thoughts. "I just want to help. You should keep an eye on the weather. Carl the weatherman on WCBV said something about a winter storm they're keeping an eye on."

"I'm from Manitoba. A tiny blizzard don't bother us none." I said it just to razz him a little since he was from Toronto. It was a thing we did. Saying Manitoba was colder and snowier than Toronto and vice versa. Just posturing a little as friends did. "But thanks for the heads up. You can go see Robbie now. I'll be fine."

"Sure, yeah, of course you will be." He blushed, then muttered something before backing out of my room. I dropped down on the bed, shoulder aching, and nudged the little wooden goalie paddle back under the bed with my heel. I hoped I wouldn't need it back home. Sometimes the unseen was stronger around my parents for some bizarre reason. And this time, I couldn't rely on Christian to hold onto when the nightmares came for me because I doubted he'd even talk to me.

TWO

Christian

MITCHELL WAS IN FULL ON ASSISTANT COACH MODE AND wasn't going to let this alone.

"Two hours to get to Marmot Gorge just to get ice time is ridiculous. How will Louis get seen by the right people if we can't even get practice time?"

"We'll figure out a way to get the roof fixed," I reassured.

"We need money."

"I understand that, but —"

"And you *know* Kyle Lourenco, and he has access to a ton of money."

I made a non-committal noise and carried on stacking the deliveries into the back of my truck. There was no way I was approaching Kyle for anything because that meant putting my head above the parapet and making myself far too vulnerable. He'd left, and I was happy with that. He'd deserved his shot at the NHL, and when Boston had taken him in the draft, there'd been no one prouder than me. I'd sent him away with a kiss and a promise that I was okay with his decision.

I'd lied.

But I'd assumed he'd come home at times, that he'd at least keep in touch, and maybe we could work at being long-distance lovers, boyfriends—hell I'd even have taken just staying friends, but the calls had become texts, and the visits had dwindled, until one day we just stopped talking. It wasn't deliberate. I don't remember the exact day I'd realized that I was Kyle's past and that I had to live with it.

How could I compare to the NHL, the fame, the money, and the internal drive he had to be the best goalie out of Manitoba since Terry Sawchuk made his way to the Redwings from Winnipeg in forty-nine? I was just the guy back home who went from best friend to friend-with-benefits to ex-friend; and so no, I wouldn't be calling Kyle and asking if he wanted to fundraise for the Eagle Ridge Eaglets, the team I coached.

"Nope." I gave Mitchell my answer, and he cursed under his breath.

"He's Eagle Ridge born and bred." Mitchell slammed his toque down over his curls in frustration. "He would help at the drop of the hat if you asked him."

Since we hadn't spoken in a long time, I doubt that. He'd left, I stayed, and it wasn't going to be fixed any time soon, so I couldn't just casually call and ask for a donation or even spread the word to his team.

"We'll manage," I lied. Somehow, I'd get up on the

roof myself and mend the hole currently hidden by the temporary fix of nailed wood.

Only, if the promised storm hit today and snow piled up, then that could be the roof gone. Not that I had time to worry about the after-effects of the storm, because I was loading my truck with final groceries and essentials to get out to people in town that needed it. I needed to worry about the deliveries now, and shelve everything else.

"Maybe I'll ask his parents to call him," Mitchell said, as if the idea had only just occurred to him.

"Leave them alone," I warned and turned to face Mitchell so he could see the intention in my eyes. "Don't mess with their heads like that." Kyle's mom, Miriam, and Patrick, her husband of forty years, made the best of everything and never once complained that they never saw Kyle. The whole town, all two thousand and four souls, plus anyone within driving distance, knew that Kyle was two things: an NHL star they were vocally proud of and an absent son. Most of the time, it was easy for others to forget the second part, but for me, the one who helped his parents, I couldn't reconcile the Kyle I thought I'd known, with the man he'd become.

Mitchell gave a heavy sigh, then nodded.

A heavy gust of wind battered the front windows of Gauthier Stores, and we both glanced out as the first snow today began to flutter down.

"I need to finish up, Mitch," I encouraged him out of the store. He was mumbling about money and rinks as he stalked outside. I knew he wanted the best for his son—so did I—because Louis was sparky and fast, and I had this feeling we'd be losing him soon to the Ice Caps out of Marmot Gorge. I seriously wanted the best for him.

Maybe after Christmas, I could send the Boston team a general email, not even mentioning who I was, and then they could fundraise or donate, and I wouldn't even have to talk to Kyle.

Maybe not.

I pulled the blinds and locked the door. We were four days from Christmas, and with the storm threatening to cut us off, this could be the last time in a while I'd see the store, at least until after Christmas Day. I had four big drops to make, the final ones today, and then I was heading back to my cabin.

My last delivery of the day was to the Edwards family, all ten of them, in a rambling farmhouse, from great grandparents to the littlest of them all—baby Emille. They'd put in a big order, enough to keep them fed and happy through any storm that might isolate them. I'd only just dropped off everything and somehow avoided being dragged in for an Edwards family Christmas, when a familiar truck slid toward me coming from the direction of town.

Mitchell. If he was going to go on about approaching Kyle for money again, then I would lose my shit. The truck fishtailed to a stop next to mine, and I rolled down the window, frigid air blasting my face and a bucket of snow whitening my coat.

"Louis! Amy! Eagle Bluff! Hannah says they haven't come home!"

In a millisecond, I switched from store owner and team coach, to search and rescue mode, and I shoved my truck in drive and headed up the old logging road. Eagle Bluff was a natural overlook for the town, with a small lake that froze at the first sign of cold and become a popular place for the team to go skating. I called the incident in, unfortunately help was at least sixty out, so it was just me against whatever was up there. Mitchell was right behind me, but I lost him in the swirling snow, and visibility was worsening the further I drove, until finally I reached the off-road parking area and killed the engine. My kit was in the back. From ropes to med-bag, I yanked it out as Mitchell pulled in next to me and jumped out. He was dressed for snow, but his Canada Goose coat wouldn't help if the kids were in the water or hanging off the bluff.

"Stay here," I ordered him, but he wasn't listening, gripping the guide rope I attached to my truck, the one also linked to my belt. It was a thin connection between me and an anchor point so I could find my way back to the truck. I was confident it would reach the pond just beyond the parking, but I could only hope the kids weren't in trouble any further than the pond and outlook itself.

"Coming with you!" he shouted over the ferocious roar of wind forcing bullets of ice at any uncovered piece of skin.

"Hold the rope!" I shouted because arguing with anyone from Eagle Ridge was a lost cause, since everyone here had experience in the extremes. I yanked him closer to me, and slowly, we followed the trees until they opened up. Not being able to see any further than a foot or so in front of me, I stopped walking, quieting the panic and forcing myself to think clearly. I pictured the small lake, barely more than a shallow pond really, and the boulders where the kids would sit to stare at the view. Louis was with Amy, his girlfriend, which meant this wasn't about skating, but probably more about making out.

For fuck's sake.

Did no one watch the weather reports?

I took a couple of experimental steps into the trees, where at least the snow was blocked by the broad trunks of old black spruce and jack pine, and got my first look at what I faced. I couldn't see the kids, but I could make out the boulders on the edge of the bluff. It was there that I headed, marking each tree, unrolling the guide rope, and pushing through the freezing gale until I reached the first rock. I could see a shape hunched by the giant stone and knew that was my first objective.

"Stay next to the tree," I shouted at Mitchell. "I'll bring them here."

The first shape was Amy, cradling herself and hunkered down with as much cover as she could get. I couldn't talk to her over the noise here, a cacophony of wind and storm shoving and biting at us. She pointed over the edge, her eyes wide with fear, and I hooked her hand to the rope. I could let her go back to the trees on her own, but if she let go of the guide, she could end up lost.

Instead, I stumbled back with her to where Mitchell was and left her with him before stepping back out into the icy hell. I headed to the boulders again, to the edge, and sank to my knees, feeling for the edge of the bluff, then laying down—thanking the heavens for waterproof clothes—and staring through the white to locate Louis. He could be gone. The fall from here was fifty feet down in a sharp drop, and if he'd gone over the side, then this could be all about recovery.

I thought I heard something—a yell—my name—help —and when the wind lessened for a moment, I saw Louis. Miraculously, he'd fallen into Bent Tree. Named by generations before me, it was an impossible aspen growing at forty-five degrees, stubbornly clinging to the cliff and the scrubby soil there. No one climbed on it, no one touched it, and it remained through all these generations just to capture Louis in his fall, like a small object in a giant skeleton hand. I snaked closer to the edge, digging the crampon into the rock—the hammer an impossible weight in my hand—and tying off the guide rope and the heavy rescue rope. I inched a harness down to him, getting as close to the edge as I could, but he couldn't grab it; frozen in place, sheltered by the branches, but probably heading towards hypothermia, if he didn't have it already.

I considered all the options, knocked in another crampon as efficiently as possible, then pulled on a harness and sent a prayer to anyone listening. I lowered myself over the edge, belaying the rope until I was closer to him. Bent Tree had saved his life, not only cradling him in skeletal fingers, but keeping him out of the worst of the storm. Even though he was wearing a bulky coat, I somehow got the twin harness on him. His eyes were open as we worked together. After a few aborted starts, we got back up, slowing as we left the shelter of Bent Tree and ended up in the wild of the storm. They certainly hadn't exaggerated how it would hit the area, and I hoped no one else was out in this. We reached the top, and I gave him one last shove to get him up and over, and then scrambled to get up myself, unhooking the twin harness from him and reaching for his arm.

A sudden blast of ice shoved at me, and for a second of horror, I was hanging over the edge, flailing until the rope tightened and Mitchell was there, yanking me back. Between us, we made it to the trees, following the guide rope—with Louis leaning onto his dad for support—back to the parking area. A scarlet rescue truck pulled in next to us, and within ten minutes, both kids were in the back, and we were leaving. They'd be okay, frostbitten and hypothermic, but alive and smiling in relief. Mitchell grasped me into a bro-hug, and then after loading up, our convoy headed down. I was still on call for emergencies, but it wasn't long after the rescue truck vanished that the road was deemed impassable. I headed through town to my cabin in the woods, pulling my vehicle into the warm oversized garage and shutting the door on the gale.

The first point of order was refitting the truck, checking the safety equipment, and sending in a report that might not make it out before the rescue truck made it to the hospital. I piled all the wet emergency gear over driers and wiped down what needed to be dried. Then I repacked everything onto the snowmobile parked in the same garage. Given my truck was going nowhere until the storm abated, the Arctic Cat would be my only choice, and I would be ready.

Finally, as warmth began seeping into my bones, I took a moment to reflect on that single deathly moment where I could have fallen back into nothing. I couldn't have relied on Bent Tree catching me. I couldn't say that I would have made it back alive, and it was as chilling as ice pellets thinking I could have died.

After I allowed myself that single black thought, I stretched out sore muscles and wiped at my face where Bent Tree's icy limbs had sliced at me. At least there was no blood, but I bet I'd have a black eye.

Heading into the main house through the connecting door, I added wood to the stove and made coffee, and only after my caffeine levels were high enough to get me moving did I take a shower. I changed into sweats and a T-shirt, warm and cozy in my place, ready to sit and read, with the sound of the storm raging around me and the emergency radio on the table next to me in case I was needed.

The heavy thump on my door broke through the snow and wind, and I couldn't help thinking I'd have repairs if the storm had thrown something like a branch at it.

Only there was another thump.

And another.

THREE

Kyle

Growing up this far north—only an hour or so away from my mother's homeland of Nunavut—my mother probably envisioned all kinds of bloody deaths for me as a child. I was kind of rambunctious. Christian had been too. Guess that was what being a ten-year-old boy was all about. We'd spend hours playing hockey or sledding or trying to sneak up on seal holes when Hudson Bay froze over in the winter. In the summer, we'd take an old handmade canoe that had belonged to my grandfather out into the bay to try to harpoon the beluga whales that swam into the bay to calf. We never did spear a whale with our sharpened sticks and clothesline whaling devices. Actually, the only time we were close to a whale—one breached about ten feet from our ratty canoe—we about shit our shorts and never went whaling again. I blame our English teacher for making us read *Moby Dick*.

Mom and Mrs. Gauthier both used to whisper thanks to

the Gods when we'd come home half-frozen or soaked to the skin, filled with tales of adventures. They were sure we'd end up in a polar bear's belly, or inside a whale, or simply kidnapped by the influx of birders who flocked to the area from May to August.

Neither of our moms would have pulled over to take a piss. And certainly they wouldn't have poked their noses over the bluff that overlooked the Friesen pond and started a conversation with the local survivalist who'd been armed to the teeth. This area held so many memories for me I tended to get lost in them at times. And I bet neither of them would have been unlucky enough to come face to face with Clyde Friesen, aka Loony Clyde, who was patrolling his land as if he expected an army to invade. I'd listened to him ranting from his side of a high barbwire fence that now stopped anyone getting to the river for fishing—something vague and just out of reach or... I don't even know. I'd been rooted to the spot, and when he stopped talking to me and then simply stared, his head slightly tilted, his rifle raised, that was when I fucked off as fast as I could.

I bet Mom and Mrs. Gauthier never entertained the notion that I'd end up dead from veering to miss a fucking moose in the road during a blizzard and running off the road and smack into a tree. Well, maybe Mom *did* consider that. She always used to say, "Drive carefully and watch for the moose!" when I'd finally gotten my license. Mom seemed to worry more than most mothers, but that was probably due to me having such disturbing dreams as a child.

I should have been paying attention to my surroundings, instead of daydreaming about sneaking onto Clyde's property to catch yellow perch with Christian or pondering over how little the airstrip at Marmot Gorge had changed.

It couldn't be called an airport. That would mean they had a building or two. All Rocky Qappik had was a crop-dusting plane and an overgrown mile of blacktop that used to lead to a bar that had burned down in the fifties. Logan International it was not, but I wasn't going to be snooty. Rocky had flown in to pick me up at Churchill Airport as the storm blew in. I owed him big time and paid him double for the harrowing half-hour flight. Rocky was going to be pissed when he saw what I'd done to his wife's, aka loan/rental, vehicle.

After the accident, which was a whole four-seconds of terror, wrenching on the wheel of the rental SUV and pumping the brakes, I sat there in the Ford Explorer dazed as snow piled up on the windshield at an alarming rate. My newly mended shoulder was on fire, the snap of the seatbelt and the detonation of the airbags ripping the external stitches out by the feel of it. My head had bounced off the side window after bouncing off the deployed airbag and was leaking blood. There was no sign of concussion. I knew what they felt like. I'd had two already in my hockey career. My neck was sore as hell, but other than the cut on my head, a few ripped sutures, and a stiff neck, I seemed to be fine.

It took me a few moments to clear my head and make an assessment. Other than my shoulder, I was okay. Sore and trembling, but safe. Thank God for seatbelts. If I'd not been strapped in, I would have been flying through the windshield and kissing a tree. That thought made me queasy. I tried the windshield wipers. They made one pass, then died. It was just enough to see that the front of the Explorer was bent around a fat fir tree.

"Great," I moaned, easing my right hand down to free myself from the seatbelt. Powder from the airbags filled the interior, making me cough and sputter. The headlights were still on. Which was good. Sitting here in the woods alone in the dark made me edgy. The unseen could be lurking in the forest, silent, like the wolves that prowled the muskeg, forests, and tundra of Manitoba. There was plenty around home that could kill you that didn't dwell in your nightmares. "Fucking great." I checked my phone for service, even though I knew there wouldn't be any this far from Eagle Ridge during a blizzard. "Fuck," I snarled, which ignited a new pain in my neck. Super, so I now had whiplash, as well as a re-fucked shoulder. "Asshole moose."

I knew the area well. I had to get somewhere warm and call for a tow truck. There was little to be done for my shoulder. That would have to wait until I could get to Churchill where they had a pretty decent health center. It would set me back a few weeks. I gave it another ten minutes, then my headlights began to dim. A deep, unsettling unease crept into my chest. Without the lights on the dash or the headlights, the darkness would descend.

Grabbing my Rebels duffel, my childhood stick, and the bag of presents for my parents, I took the keys from the ignition and exited the car. Snow whipped around me, tiny bits of ice mixing in with the flakes to scour any exposed skin. Thankfully, I had worn my thickest winter coat. The son of Miriam Enook Lourenco knew enough to dress in layers. Shame he didn't know enough to not run off the damn road. Fear spurred me on. The wind was brutally cold. The outside temperature, according to the dash of Rocky's totaled SUV, had read zero degrees Fahrenheit, which was normal for this time of year. I took a few steps, my hood cinched around my head, and turned on the flashlight that had been in the car, to give me about a foot of light before the snow cut the beam into nothingness. I swallowed. It was fine. I knew where I was. Christian had a cabin just a mile or so down Egret Lane. Head down, I pushed into the storm, the snow already to my knees.

Once I got into the woods, the wind did ease a bit, but not enough. Something cracked behind me. I spun around with a gasp, heart pounding in my chest, and waved the light back and forth.

"Who is it?" I shouted, but the gale force winds carried my words away. I stood there, locked in fear, snow battering my face like a sandblaster, squinting to see into the maelstrom.

Just a tree. It was just a tree breaking and falling.

Nothing to worry about. It's not the unseen. Just keep walking. You know this road. Round the bend. Up the knoll. The old Adjuk place. Mom told you all about it. Dad helped Christian put on a new roof when he bought it. You're safe, just keep walking.

"Safe is a relative term," I whispered into the night. Safe from the thing in the dark? Maybe. Safe from falling trees, polar bears, wolves, wandering moose? Not so much. But if I stopped moving and gave into the fear, I'd freeze to death here within thirty minutes. Windchill and exposure came fast. My jeans were already soaked, my thighs burning from the cold. My hiking boots were full of snow, my toes icy cold. Maybe the son of Miriam Enook Lourenco wasn't all that clever after all. I should have worn snow boots, but I hated driving in clunky shoes.

Feeling the dread roost on my shoulder, I turned back the way I had been going. The small road was snowed in, and if not for the soft and subtle dip where the drainage ditches ran, you wouldn't know the road from the woods. Shoulder up, the other was tight to my side, because I'd removed the sling when I'd used the men's room at the Churchill Airport and had forgotten to put it back on.

Accidentally forgot or forgot on purpose?

Shut up. Focus on getting to the Adjuk cabin.

A mile doesn't seem long when it's a warm sunny day. We had those here in Eagle Ridge. In the summer, the daylight seemed to go on forever. In the winter, we had around sixteen hours of darkness, and only eight of light. It made for some long ass nights. Perhaps once the storm passed, and if I survived long enough to reach Christian's cabin, I'd be able to see the Northern Lights. A memory overtook me as I trudged along, one cold foot in front of the other, of a time that seemed like a lifetime ago, but was only really about nine years.

Christian and I lying in the snow behind his house, bundled up, watching the dancing red, blue, and green streaks shimmering in the arctic sky. *Aqsarniit*, my mother called it. We boys called it magical. We spun stories about mythical monsters or airships that ran on the energy of the Lights. That night, we were fifteen, and we held hands as we lay in the deep snow, our sight on the skies. Even though we were wearing gloves, it was one of the defining moments of my life.

It was the night when Christian had told me he liked boys. I'd known I was crushing on my best friend for well over a year. I'd worked out that I was gay when I was thirteen, but kept that secret locked down tight. The other boys always said they didn't want fags in the locker room with them, although I doubted they even knew exactly what that term meant at that age. I certainly didn't. It was only when I started to find Christian so appealing that I began to wonder about myself. Why hadn't I thought any of the girls around town were as beautiful as my best friend? When he finally grasped my hand that night, my world flipped upside down. I lay there too scared to move in case he let go of my hand.

He rolled to his side and stole a kiss. It was brief and chaste, a mere brush of his cold lips over mine, but it was *everything.* He was the only boy I had kissed. And he would remain the only man that I wanted to kiss. Even right now, half frozen with only a scant flow of light to keep the unseen at bay, I had no desire to lock lips with another man. If the shadowy shape took me now, I'd die happy, knowing that I had loved one person wholly. And how we had loved.

We discovered each other in the summers that followed that cold kiss under the dancing lights. Slowly, and with shaky trepidation, we began exploring each other's bodies as the years raced past. In our senior year, we finally became lovers. He was gentle and sweet when he first entered me. It hurt a little. We were both fumbling fools with only the barest knowledge of how sex with two men really worked. That kind of thing wasn't exactly discussed in our health classes at Eagle Ridge High. We were lucky to get a basic course on human anatomy in ninth grade. Abstinence was the preferred sexual education policy. Gay sex wasn't even mentioned, other than a brief side note about homosexuality, where all the guys sniggered.

A branch fell in front of me with a crack as loud as a starter's gun. I yelped, pulled from the past instantly. Fear lodged in my throat as my heart thudded loudly against my ribs.

"Fuck," I panted, shaking free of the spell of all those memories. I looked from the rotted limb down the dark lane. If I just kept moving, the bend in the road would be soon. I moved on, the ache in my shoulder growing with each step. A pine tree lay across the road at the bend. I climbed over it, the exertion making my shoulder scream. I could feel the blood wetting my shirt.

God I was stupid. Stupid Kyle. Stupid moose. Stupid storm. I should have just stayed in Boston like everyone wanted me to, but no, I had to bull ahead. Bull. Ha. Yeah, moose. Bull. Rocky. It all goes together. Maybe it's a short Russian guy named Boris lurking around in my dreams. That's funny shit.

Not really. Stop giggling and keep moving.

I wondered how long it took for delirium to set in after a car wreck and a stroll through a blizzard. Not long I bet. That stupid Bullwinkle crack was a sure sign I was walking a fine line between calm and panic.

My gaze darting left and right, I pushed on, the snow making each step harder and harder. If I hadn't been in top shape, I wasn't sure I would have made it this far. The wind howled through the forest, calling out long forgotten names of mystical creatures. Maybe it was a *Taqriaqsuit* that haunted me. Mom talked of the shadow people who were rarely seen, but often heard on gusts of wind. She had even talked about my nightmares with my father, and that word had been whispered. Mom carried a great deal of her heritage with her, filling my head with tales of monsters that snatched children into the sea or a demon that prowls the Arctic and tickles its victims to death. If one of the shadow people was what I saw at night, all the good omens in the world wouldn't save me from a hideous fate. And that would suck. I was too young to die. I'd never get to see Christian again, or taste his lips, or feel him moving inside me.

Then get moving. He's right there! Look away from the snow and see the light!

Raising my sight, I spied the light. It was small and nearly obscured by the lashing snow, but it was there. The crush of the unseen—the shadow man who stalked me—started to recede. I tried to run, but the snow slowed me. Eyes locked on that icy window, I plodded on, aching and bitterly cold, until I crested the knoll.

I made it to the front door and gave it a kick. A whimper escaped me. I kicked the door again and then again. Finally, it opened. And there he was. Christian.

My Christian.

Nothing that moved on this realm or the next was as glorious as Christian Gauthier. Stunned to his core, yes, but still breathtaking.

"Christian… I need… you… help," I croaked, then fell into his arms.

FOUR

Christian

Somewhere between shock and the blast of snow that hit me in the face, I realized that Kyle Lourenco was on my front porch, and in a heartbeat, my training kicked in. I caught him as he fell forward and somehow managed to angle him so that I could lift him inside. He'd never been a small guy, but barely conscious and weighed down by his coat, a duffel, and a shit ton of snow, he was deadweight. I had to avoid excessive movements, knowing this may trigger cardiac arrest in even the healthiest of guys, but he was no small thing I could scoop up in my arms. An entire list of questions formed in my head, and it was only my experience that allowed me to focus.

I ran a hundred things through my head. I knew he'd been injured, and not just because local news had the incident on repeat, but because Mom told me so, followed by my sister, then with half the town talking about it in the store. Upper body injury the team said, but that could have meant anything—was he out of playing because of a concussion? What was he doing out in the snow? Why was he bleeding? Why wasn't he safely at his parent's place where I could safely not see him at all? I know they'd been surprised he was coming home for Christmas after all this time, but it seemed as if he hadn't even made it there. Had he wrecked his car? I leaned back against the door, forcing it closed against the storm, and finally he was out of the cold.

"Kyle?" I was stuck, unable to think, and he was icy against me. *Think. Think.*

Lie him down, somewhere warm, and dry; get him out of the wet clothing, cut it off if I need to; and avoid excess movement. The bed seemed like the best place, and it was the door closest to me. I moved him through the door and attempted to get his coat off. Thankfully, that part was easy enough—although he cried out in pain—even if his eyes were shut and his breathing was harsh.

I lay him back on the bed as gently as I could, darting out to the kitchen and grabbing my med kit, then hurried back in. He hadn't moved, sprawled on my bed, his chest rising and falling as he breathed, his skin pale. I couldn't take off his toque easily because there was blood on his face that had soaked into the material, so I cut around it to remove the wet material. His jeans went the same way, removed cautiously and with the judicious use of the scissors and my pocketknife. I cut away his shirt, the layers, even his underwear, until he was naked as the day he was born, and so still and pale I thought I'd lost him.

"Not losing you like this, asshole," I muttered and grabbed all the blankets I had and piled them over him. I tucked them in and around him while trying to ignore the wound in his shoulder that was puffy and red, covering him from head to toe in warmth with only his face exposed. I knew I couldn't do a damn thing about his shoulder, or the cut on his head, not yet—but at least the bleeding had stopped. The shoulder wound made sense with the whole upper body injury. I checked his pupils, and they were equal and reactive, and only he could tell me if he'd been under concussion protocol, but I couldn't exactly shake him awake and ask him.

"Kyle, are you with me?"

He murmured something, his lips moving, but his eyes remaining shut. I don't know how long he'd been in the snow, but relief flowed through me knowing it hadn't been long enough to push him into the severest level of hypothermia. Yes, he was unconscious, but he had a pulse and was breathing. Leaving the bedroom door open, I hurried back to the kitchen and made hot chocolate—the only sweet beverage I could think of—and took the drink into the room, then went back out to find something to act as a warm compress. I had fluid-filled bags in my med kit that warmed when squeezed, but I had an entire damn kitchen here, and after a few moments of irrational dazed panic, I finally pulled out hot water bottles and filled them with barely warm water. Only when I had them placed on Kyle's neck, chest, and groin, and had covered him with the blankets, did I have a chance to stop and think. There was nothing else I could do for him now—time would tell me if he was going to be okay.

The instincts and training that had guided me this far and let me treat the man at my door with professional focus slowly slipped away. Panic took their place momentarily until I wrangled fright into submission and finally sunk to the seat in the corner of the room and simply stared at him.

I should use the radio and contact his parents—let them know where he was, and that he was okay—because they were probably concerned that he hadn't turned up. I should report him being here to the search and rescue team. Maybe I should call the RCMP. Someone might be looking for him, a friend, a lover? There might be someone else in the car wreck I assume he'd walked away from.

I couldn't move as shock stole my rational thoughts, and I needed to know whether I had to go out there and rescue someone else.

"Kyle, were you alone?" No response, and then his eyes opened a little and I got my first look at the inky depths of a man in pain. "Is there someone else out there in the snow?" I asked clearly.

"Huh?"

"Were you alone in the car?"

"Car?"

"Is anyone else in danger?"

"Alone," he managed and closed his eyes again. That was one thing I guess—he'd been driving in a snowstorm on his own, which meant I didn't need to suit up and get out there. He'd slipped back into sleep, but it was restless and jarring as he groaned in pain and mumbled something that I barely made out… *Taqriaqsuit*. A nightmare then because the ancient phantoms of his momma's stories visited in his sleep, and I'd held him before when the night terrors consumed him. I'd held him and quieted his fears, and he'd left me, and he'd never come back.

"No… no… no…"

The blankets moved a little as he jerked and then whimpered, but his eyes were still closed, and I knew he wasn't in this world right now. Wherever he was, he was fighting the same age-old demons that plagued his childhood. There was only one thing that stopped them then, but it meant me climbing into bed with him and cradling him, reassuring him I could keep him safe. It meant me opening my heart to the only man I loved and promising him I'd be there forever.

I refused to lie because forever was something we'd never have.

I stroked his face gently, fingers catching the coarse stubble there, and stilling at his cheekbones, wondering how a face so dear to me could make me react so badly. I wanted to shout at him, rail at him for disappearing on us all, and it didn't matter how much I'd loved him… we were over. He quietened after a moment, his lips moving as if he was trying to fashion words, but I left him and headed for the radio system in the small office room off the kitchen. I spoke to the sheriff's department, then left details with the health center over in Churchill, getting their list of things I needed to do, which was handed out to me in a well-practiced speech. This kind of thing happened often, just not to locals like Kyle, who knew this part of the world better than most. How had he wrecked a car on roads he knew like the back of his hand? What pulled him to my door? Was he even a local anymore now that he'd taken himself and his heart down to Boston?

I was only left with contacting his parents, Miriam and Patrick, and that was going to be the hardest connection of all. Last time I saw Miriam was when I delivered out to their place, maybe three days back. Patrick took in the delivery, but Miriam had come to the door. She'd been cheery about the upcoming holiday. Was that why Kyle had come home—to celebrate? And why now? He hadn't been home for Christmas—or any other major holiday—for years. I get he's part of a team, and that he can't just drop everything, but that was what the summer break was for. Right? That short period over the summer was surely the one time he could have come home to see them.

And me.

Patrick answered the call as soon as I placed it. I pictured the radio in their front room, right by the easy chair that I would sometimes sit in to watch hockey games with him. I was never there for games where I'd see Kyle, and if Patrick ever realized I always had an excuse whenever the local channels covered the Boston team coming this far north, then he never called me on it. He was a good man who saw more than he let on.

"Hello, Christian, this is Patrick, over."

"Patrick, I have Kyle here with me, in case you were worried. Over."

There was a pause and then a crackle. "Say again. Over."

"Patrick, I have Kyle here with me, in case you were worried. Over."

More crackles and then all pretense at following radio etiquette was out of the window, and I could hear the shock in Patrick's voice.

"Kyle. Our Kyle? Why is he at your place?" Radio etiquette had stopped, and he'd cut straight to the questions.

I waited a few seconds, not just in case he wanted to say more, but also to give myself time to think about what to say next. I'd already decided to keep the details brief, explain he was sleeping and cold, but that I had everything in hand.

"He came to my door from an accident in his car. He's okay, but he's sleeping. I'll get him to you as soon as I can, over."

"We thought he'd stopped back in town," Patrick sounded bewildered. "He should have pulled off the road and gotten out of the storm." I heard some talking. Kyle's mom was asking questions. "Is he hurt?" Patrick summarized.

"He's okay," I lied. "Just warming him up."

"We were so happy he was coming to Eagle Ridge." Patrick was still in shock. "It's been so long since he's been home."

Kyle ghosted in and out of people's lives as if nothing mattered to him, and I could hear the confusion in Patrick's voice over the fact his son was coming home at all, let alone coming home and crashing his car like a tourist. Kyle knew these roads. Why had he been so stupid? He'd paid for his parents to go to Boston for an extended vacation back in February, but not coming home, not wanting to see any of us here, was his default. His parents excused it as him being busy, but I knew the one big thing that kept him from coming here—the phantoms that stole his happy, and most of all, his pathological need to avoid me.

"I'll get him to contact you when he wakes up. Keep him here until the storm eases. Over."

"Should we be worried? Over." The last thing that Patrick and Miriam needed was fear for their idiot son.

"No. Over."

"Keep us in the loop, Christian, thank you. Over."

"My love to Miriam. Over."

With all that done, I headed straight back to Kyle. Was he finally visiting his parents because he was injured and needed them? Or the town? *Or me?* And why after all this time? Taking my own hot chocolate into the bedroom, I stood for a while at the end of the bed and stared down at Kyle. From what I'd seen in the panicked moments of getting him in here, he'd filled out more since I knew him, broader, more muscled; hell he'd always been a rangy kid, bendy and athletic, but now he was a man. The pictures on the television, or the internet, didn't do him justice. Most of the time he was buried in his goalie gear, which hid all of him.

Not that I'd been looking.

Liar.

"Don't hurt me…" he mumbled, moved a little under the covers, and his lips parted on a keening wail that made the hairs on my arms stand up. There was a stark terror in the noise that made me clamber onto the bed because whatever he was to me now—he used to be my best friend —he needed something that I'd been the only one to ever be able to give him. "Please, don't hurt me… no!" he gasped, and tears leaked out of his eyes, his breathing harsher. I moved closer, bringing the small med kit with me, and cradled his head, making sure the blankets remained tucked around him. He immediately quieted at my touch, and muttered something else, before trying to turn his head, seeking my touch, and moaning in pain. I smoothed his long dark hair from his forehead and tucked the blankets to hide it, and then gently dabbed the antiseptic on the part of the toque still stuck to his wound. After a moment or two, the material eased, and I got my first look at what had happened to his head. It wasn't as bad as I feared—a surface wound that would need stitches, but had actually stopped bleeding.

Cleaning the area, I applied tiny butterfly bandages to the wound, and then, there was nothing else I could do except wait. I reached out for my book, a biography about Errol Flynn, and lost myself in the Golden Age of Hollywood, as my hand rested on his head, his breathing measured, and thankfully, no more dreams about phantoms out to kill him. I was up to 1938 and *The Adventures of Robin Hood* when Kyle moved against my hand and opened his eyes.

"Wh'appen?" he managed, then groaned in pain. I had something for that, and I eased his head up, supported him, and got him to swallow meds. The hot chocolate was long cold, but it was sweet, and I encouraged him to drink some of that as well, even though he grimaced. There was nothing else to do medically, and now it was just two men half lying on a bed in awkward silence.

"Christian?" he whispered. "What happened?"

"You tell me," I said with a sigh. "I assume you ran off the road and walked here."

"Hurts," he managed, then screwed his eyes tight, not saying anything else. From the way he clenched his jaw, the pain was intolerable. I let him lie still until I could see him relaxing as the meds began to work. He pushed at the blankets. I touched his skin, and he was warmer, so I didn't push them back as tight as they had been, just settled them loosely over him up to his neck.

"Shit," he moaned, attempted to move, and then whimpered under his breath, and the tears started again, trickling from his closed eyes and tracking down his face, soaking into the blankets. Just as quickly as they started, they stopped, and I went back to Robin Hood as he slept peacefully next to me—no more nightmares.

Darkness still had the land in its grip when he woke again, and this time, I helped him sit upright in the bed and tucked the blankets around him, which he pushed away with stubborn focus.

"M'okay." He stared at me mutinously, but I knew what was best for him right now, and I wasn't taking any shit.

"You're far from okay, idiot."

"Moose," he grumbled, and he didn't have to expand. Around here just the word moose explained so much. Likely it had been on the road, and he'd either hit it or swerved to avoid it, probably not having any chance of stopping his car.

"RCMP is aware of an accident, but we're in a whiteout right now."

His eyes widened. "Mom. Dad. I need to—"

"I told them you were here, and they were surprised to hear you'd run off the road, let alone that you were traveling in a snowstorm."

He wouldn't meet my gaze, shifting on the bed and wincing before sighing. "Fucked that up," he said quietly. "Got delayed. I pulled off the road, took too long staring at…" He stopped talking and groaned in pain.

"You have a habit of fucking up when it comes to family." Sarcasm slipped into my tone, and I didn't stop it from spilling out. The first time I'd seen my former best friend and lover in years, and all the pent-up frustration was right there waiting to get its chance in the light. "What was so damn important to get here after all this time that you chance your safety like that?"

"It's snow, I *know* snow," he defended, his voice cracking.

"Snow kills," I snapped. "Idiot." Hell, I was still shaky with what had happened at Bent Tree, the image of being suspended over swirling white would haunt me for a long time. If I'd been there alone, I would have fallen, and even though the rope might have held me, I would have been injured, in need of saving myself.

"No, moose kill," he corrected me and winced again, trying to get himself to a more comfortable position. "Fuck."

I stopped his movements with a hand to his chest, holding him still. "What are you doing here, Kyle? Why now?"

FIVE

Kyle
———

"You have a habit of fucking up when it comes to family."

Well ouch. That was brutally honest. I wasn't sure what hurt worse, the slam from Christian, my shoulder, or my head. Probably the slam. My shoulder and head would heal eventually. Knowing that Christian thought so little of me would take eons to scab over, if it ever did. His hand on my chest felt good, safe. That was one thing about him that I adored. That feeling of security he carried with him like a warm blanket and a hot toddy. Always at the ready to protect and heal, even if the people he was rescuing didn't deserve his kindness.

"Are you sure you're not concussed?" he asked with a softness that had been lacking just a moment ago. I should have said I was concussed, just so he'd be kinder to me, but I didn't really deserve his compassion.

"I'm sure. I know what they feel like." I pushed up to

get the stress off my lower back. His hand fell away, leaving me feeling alone once more.

"Yeah, and how did that work for you," he muttered as he left the bed and exited the room. My eyes couldn't leave him until he was out of sight. God, he was beautiful, even more appealing now than when he'd been younger. A few years had added a maturity to his features. He was a man now. A man with a grudge that was fully justified. I threw back the covers, wincing at the movement, the cooler air wafting over my nakedness. A rush of embarrassment raced over me. He'd seen me naked.

He's seen you naked before, gumnuts.

Great, now Moral's voice was bouncing around inside my head. Gumnuts. Perfect. That described me to a tee, even though I had no clue what a gumnut was. Easing my naked feet out of the bed, I looked around for my clothes. Nothing. Not even my underwear. Super. I tugged the spread from the mattress and wrapped myself up in the homemade quilt. It smelled of fabric softener and Christian. The hardwood floors were cold. I tried stepping from throw rug to throw rug, but soon ran out and had to cross the wide expanse of the living room to the small, but toasty, kitchen. Christian was at the stove stirring something in a cast iron kettle while muttering under his breath.

I cleared my throat. His green gaze flew from the pot on the gas range to me in the doorway.

"Why are you out of bed?" he asked, turning from the

food. The aroma of halibut stew hit my nose. My stomach rumbled.

"I want to get to my folks. I've not been able to be home for Christmas in years," I timidly explained.

"Five."

"Pardon?"

"Five years. You've not been home for Christmas in five years. Or home at all actually."

"Have you been keeping track?"

"Fuck no, your mom told me about every single year in detail when I dropped off some supplies a few weeks ago."

I couldn't help wincing. Not just that my mom kept track, but that his tone was dripping with sarcasm. Why did I even think that Christian might keep track of my visits to Eagle Ridge? I'd left the town and the man behind without so much as an explanation. To be honest, I wasn't even sure I knew why I had distanced myself from the people I cared about the most. There was something about coming home that made me feel uneasy. Something about the dark woods and the endless nights of winter stirred up a primal fear that seemed to reside in the marrow of my bones. No matter how far I got from Hudson Bay, the disquiet lingered, but was manageable. The problem was I thought I could escape the phantoms by staying in Boston and yet, they'd followed me there. Now that I was close to home…

My gaze flew to the small window. Nothing but snow and ice. The hairs on the back of my neck lay back down.

"What happened to your face?" I pointed at him in an effort to change the subject.

Christian touched the bruise near his eye. "A rescue." Then he shrugged. "So what's next?"

"Life has been busy," I finally said as I stopped staring at the blizzard and instead watched the man ladling up soup. He filled out his jeans and flannel shirt to perfection. Such a strong, rugged man. An outdoorsman at heart, Christian loved the wilderness and nature. I never could take to it like he had—the woods had too many shadows. But if he was with me, then I could at least pretend to be okay.

"So, Miriam says." He turned and walked to the small round wooden table in the corner. "Sit and eat."

"Did you use your mother's recipe or my mother's?" It fell out of my mouth before I could stop it. His eyes narrowed. "No, it's good. Fine. I love it. Can I have my underwear?"

His gaze skimmed down over me, cocooned in his grandmother's wedding quilt. "I cut everything off, but I'll find you something." He beat a hasty retreat to the short hall that led to the backdoor. I stood stock-still, eyeing the food and hot cup of cocoa, my mouth watering. I'd eaten in some of the fanciest eateries in the world. Places like LA, New York, Boston, Paris, Tokyo, Sweden, Norway, and a hundred others. But nothing looked as delicious as that old red ceramic bowl filled with pieces of halibut from the bay in a creamy base with chunks of carrot, celery, onion, and potato. He'd even added corn and peas, so it was my mother's recipe. His mother didn't use corn and peas.

"You can shower and change in the bathroom. There are towels in the linen closet right beside the bathroom door. Are you steady enough to dress yourself?" I startled a bit when he spoke and held out some neatly folded clothes. I reached for them, and one side of the blue and green quilt slid down off my shoulder. His eyes fell to the exposed flesh, and a flush warmed his stubbled cheeks. Was he remembering the taste of my skin? He'd loved to suckle on my clavicle and neck back in the day to make me gasp and squirm. Or was he simply looking at the surgery site? "I'll have to check that later to make sure the bleeding has stopped."

Yeah, medical reasons. Of course. I had to stop hoping for a sign that he still cared. He didn't. I'd left. He'd moved on. Surely, he'd dated after I'd gone off to make a name for myself. Mom and Dad never mentioned him seeing anyone. Not that there were a ton of gay guys in Eagle Ridge, but he'd never really expressed himself as exclusively gay. Maybe he was bi or pan; that would open up lots of dating possibilities. Well, maybe not *lots*, but more. There were a few single women around, but not many. Perhaps he had dated a couple of them. He'd always joked about being a "Kylesexual" when we'd been falling in love. Thinking of that term made me feel as warm inside as the pile of clothes fresh from the dryer. I glanced up from the clothing to him and our eyes locked.

The timer on the oven sounded, breaking the spell.

"Bread is ready." He coughed, spinning from me to pull a loaf of freshly baked bread from the oven. My gut roared.

I turned from the sight of him bent over and hurried to the bathroom. I needed to piss, wash up, and put on some damn clothes. My dick had obviously survived the crash and the hike without incident as it was now half-hard. It was amazing the effect that man had on me. Amazing and more than a little scary. I shuffled away before the smells of warm bread and Christian's seafaring cologne made my prick get any harder. I found the linen closet, removed a brown towel, and entered the small, but tidy, bathroom. It didn't have a tub, just a corner shower stall. The walls were round logs like the rest of the house, and the shower curtain and towels were mocha and teal. A tall, skinny window with a teal topper looked out into the woods. There was hardly any snow on the pane, the wind obviously blowing in a different direction. At times, there could be ten feet of snow out front and two inches at the back of the cabin where the bath and bedroom were. I'd seen that before with big storms. It was like walking into a different world, depending on which door you exited.

Letting the quilt slip to the floor, I took a minute to give myself a long look in the mirror. Christ. I looked like I'd been in a damn wreck.

"Moose kill," I quipped as I poked at the little white butterfly bandages Christian had used to close my head wound. Ouch. Yeah, that hurt more than a little. My grimace wrinkled my face. My fingers then fell to the sutures that had pulled loose. I peeled off the large bandage and sighed forlornly. There were three that were torn, the once neat incision now a little ragged on the one end. The bandage was crusty with dried blood. Christian would have to clean it and perhaps put a few stitches in, if he were capable of doing that.

Of course, he's capable. He's handled taking care of your aging parents better than you, hasn't he? You should just stop coming home. Let Christian tend to the folks. Maybe you should walk out into the snow and die. Join them like you were supposed to...

I tensed as the voice of the unseen whispered in my head. Fuck, it had been years since I'd heard that raspy, horrifying person. I broke into a cold sweat, my eyes wide, my pulse kicking up. Where was my goalie stick? I reached for the doorknob in a blind panic. The door opened and someone stepped into view. I threw myself at the person in the doorway, charging into Christian with a shout.

"Hey, what the fuck!" he shouted. Thankfully, he was a big guy, not quite as tall as me at six foot three, just lacking a few inches, but he was broader, built more like a fullback than a hockey goalie, who had to stay lean and nimble. He grabbed me by the shoulders, his fingers biting into my flesh, tugging on the already ruptured sutures. I hissed in pain, mortified beyond belief, and stumbled back into the bathroom with Christian steadying me as I wobbled around.

"Sorry, sorry, I thought..." I threw a look around the small room, but nothing was out of place. It was still a brown and teal bathroom. "Okay, sorry. I'm super jumpy."

He steadied me, his gaze searching mine. "Are you sure you're okay?"

I worked up a feeble laugh. "Yep, totally fine," I tossed out. It had been my standard reply when I'd gotten spooked as a teenager.

"I knocked a few times, but you never replied, so I came in. I thought you had passed out or something and were lying in here with a busted skull."

I shook my head as his grip softened, but his hands remained on my bare shoulders. "Just the one crack in my head, nothing new." Glancing up from my feet, I stared at him. "I was woolgathering. I didn't hear you knock." Now that the fear was subsiding, I felt the prickle of embarrassment standing around naked always brought on. His worry seemed to fizzle away when he too realized how close we were in this cramped bath. If he took just a step, he'd be pressed tightly to me. I'd kiss him if he got that close. I'd not be able to help myself. It had been so long since I tasted his lips.

"I wanted to tell you to… ah… you have to be careful with the plug. If you bump it with your foot it… uhm, it shuts and the stall floods."

I enjoyed the play of emotions in those jade eyes of his. "Noted."

"Right. Noted. I'll just go slice the bread." He bolted out of the bathroom like a scalded cat, the door slamming shut in his wake. I pulled in a shaky breath, closed my eyes, and breathed in and out with measured breaths. Just like every counselor I'd ever been to had advised over the years. When the shadow people came into my dreams and I'd wake up in a terror, I was supposed to breathe slowly while telling myself it was just a dream. There were no bad monsters in the shadows waiting to kill me like they had… someone. That was where the chasm appeared. And where most therapists faltered and then failed. Even the ones who tried to interpret my dreams or used hypnosis. There just no accessing any useful memories before my fifth birthday. Which many professionals had assured me was normal, if not unusual, as most people started having memories around the age of three or four. I wasn't so sure. And even if not recalling a thing until I was going on six was acceptable to them, it wasn't to me. There had to be a reason for the childhood amnesia, but no one knew what it was.

The wind gusted and blew a sheet of sleet into the window. I refused to look. Instead, I turned on the taps in the shower and got in, walling myself safely into the stall. The hot water felt so good. I lingered after scrubbing my hair and body, enjoying the warmth seeping into my core. Once the water started to chill, I cranked off the taps, stepped out, and gingerly dried off. Every inch of me ached. My head was touchy, and my shoulder was aching like a rotten tooth.

It took me forever to get dried and dressed. I ran the fingers of my right hand through my hair. The side of my face where I was cut was starting to bruise. My shoulder was puffy and red, kind of like my eyes. I needed more sleep, but if I crashed now, at only ten after seven in the morning, I'd be up all night. And those dark winter nights were long as fuck. I managed to get dressed with one arm, but it wasn't pretty. My underwear clung to my wet ass. Getting socks on with one hand was aggravating as hell. I left them all twisty. I truly did not care. I just wanted food and a bottle of Advil. Maybe a smile from Christian too, but that would be asking a lot.

Pulling on my jeans nearly made me yelp, but tough hockey player that I am, I simply bit back the sound. Yeah, I was tough. So tough that I nearly ran down Christian in a blind panic over a childhood bogeyman. I left the steamy bath to find some food.

"Should be cool enough to eat," Christian said when I entered the kitchen in my twisted socks and clinging underwear. He glanced up from buttering some bread for me. "Are you feverish?"

"No, I just can't lift my arm over my head." I felt foolish.

"Oh sure, of course." He licked the butter from his fingers and my dick took notice. Shame my head hadn't been bonked. Maybe that would knock some sense into it. He rose, walked round the table, and lifted the black and gold Rebels fleece from my hand. "Let me help. Also, you need to have that arm in a sling before you do more damage to it."

His concern should have been touching, but it was oddly chilly and painfully professional. Nodding dully, I handed over the sweatshirt. Right arm was easy. Left arm required some stretching of material and a few muffled curses from me. When my head popped through, Christian was *right there*, his gaze unfathomable.

"Let me get that sling." Off he went like Satan was nipping at his heels, and I followed him into the bathroom. I exhaled, a deep breath out filled with lingering pain, both physical and mental. He pulled out a dark blue sling with a long, adjustable strap. "I knew there was one in my search and rescue kit. I'll be as gentle as possible."

"Thanks," I answered, my gaze locking on the snowy window above the sink as he moved in close. Too close. He eased my arm into the sling part then gingerly fastened the strap. His chest brushed mine, and the backs of his fingers skittered over the nape of my neck as he arranged the strap. I could feel his body heat, smell his aftershave, and hear his ragged exhalations as he fiddled with the buckle. "Is this too tight?"

His breath danced over my ear. I bit back a groan. My gaze pinned to the snowy panes that the shifting winds had recently scoured clean.

"It's perfect," I whispered, my body humming with the need to turn and kiss his scruffy cheek. I almost did. Then something moved outside the window. A big, shadowy shape that darted out of sight.

I shouted at the top of my lungs.

SIX

Christian

I FELL BACK SO HARD THE DOOR RATTLED, AND MY FIGHT or flight went straight to fight as I crowded Kyle back against the toilet and picked up the nearest weapon I could find, a can of shaving foam that was nearly empty. God knows what I thought I would be doing with that, but rational thought had fled as soon as Kyle yelled in terror.

"What!" I shouted and brandished the can, staring wildly about me, searching for whatever had made Kyle scream.

"Outside!" he yelled again, then doubled over, unable to catch a breath as I stepped away from him and swiveled to the window to stare at the darkness beyond. When I focused, all I could see was snow on the lip of the window and swirling in the night, but other than that, there was nothing.

"What?" I ran through all the possible scenarios. No to a bear, obviously, maybe a moose? Maybe a person? The nearest cabin to here was only a quarter mile away, but no sane person would be out in this storm. "Were you alone in your car?" I snapped, my mind going to places it shouldn't, like he'd abandoned someone who was now, for some insane reason, walking around in subzero temperatures, in the midst of one of the worst storms to hit this area in years.

"Yes," he forced out and then crumpled to the floor, his back against the wall, and his head in his hands.

"What did you see? Was it a moose?" I needed to know the enemy I was facing, or if I needed to get on my cold gear and get my ass out into the storm. No one was dying on my watch, and if a human was out there and needed my help, then as sure as eggs are eggs, I was going out and finding them.

"Nothing," he whispered into his arms. "Just shadows."

My focus shifted, my fight reflex slowly receded, and I went to a crouch next to Kyle, still grasping the dollar can of foam. Slumped over, his breathing shallow, but at least the sharp fear had trickled away. I'd seen this before, woken up next to him as he struggled to breathe, sobbing in his sleep. The night terrors that plagued him were visceral, and he took a long time to settle from them, but this one seemed to have drained him of all energy, and he hadn't even been asleep. He was shaking a little, shivering, and I yanked at the fluffy purple robe on the back of the door—a present from Mom and the softest thing I owned —then encouraged him to slip it around him. It was awkward because he didn't want to leave the wall, but I finally levered him away to wrap him entirely in mauve, pulling up the soft hood of it and covering his head.

"Fuck…" He slipped out of my hold to move back against the wall, and I waited for a few seconds to see if he would look up at me.

"I thought you were seeing people about this?" How could he have a career and live in Boston if he hadn't mastered the nightmares and fear that dogged him? Maybe he had a new version of me living with him, a boyfriend, someone who held him when he cried and rocked in fear? I couldn't even think of that now. I needed to get him out of his head, and so I encouraged him to stand, or more like pulled him to his feet, then tugged and half carried him into the main sitting room, a fire burning in the fireplace, and settled him in the corner of the sofa. The blinds were all down. There was nothing to see, no one outside, but he wouldn't let go of me.

"My stick," he mumbled, and the simple words cut like a knife to my heart. He was still holding that? Sleeping with it when I couldn't be there? I immediately went to the pile of gear that he'd dropped inside the front door, and there, under the bags of gifts that he'd for some reason decided to bring through the storm with him from the car, was the kids' goalie stick. Just the sight of it made my stomach fall. Without me next to him, had he really reverted to needing this? It wasn't my place to comment, but his mom said he'd been doing so well. Miriam and Patrick were so proud of him, and hell, he was a goalie for an NHL team, he was a man who didn't know fear for hundred-mile-an-hour pucks flying at his face, yet he still had the stick? He *still* had the terror that carved into every cell of him.

I took the stick back to him, and my heart stopped when he took it from me and cradled it like a baby. The fuck? This was a grown man, one of the quickest, most focused, and agile goalies in a high-pressure game, with millions in the bank, yet sitting there, he was just the scared kid that I'd let go of.

"Come with me. I can get us a place."

I regretted saying no, but what would I be in a city as vast as Boston? The boyfriend? Just there to hold him when he was scared? Here in Eagle Ridge, I was the center of the town—people relied on me, my family, his family, all the people in town who came to my store, the tourists who visited and needed rescuing—all of this framed me as a person. I couldn't have given all of that up for one man, however much he was the other half of my heart.

But seeing him sitting there still shaking, it wasn't so much that I couldn't have left. It was that I *should* have gone with him. He called me to be his rock, his touchstone, but even with that, he'd still cut me from his life. Why? Was he so scared in Boston that he wasn't able to text me? Was his life just a new prison, but in a different place?

"Shit, Kyle." I crouched next to him, my adrenaline rush subsiding, and suddenly feeling as if my entire life had changed in a millisecond. "Tell me you don't still sleep with that thing."

He shook his head, and for a moment I was relieved that I was wrong, and then he spoke and my life shifted again in an instant.

"It's the only thing that stops the nightmares," he murmured.

"I thought you were seeing someone, seeing people, to talk about it all."

"I am. Every three weeks I sit in the room with the counselor, and we talk about my goddamn life and how much opportunity I have, and how lucky I am, and how fucking good I am at my fucking goddamn job!" He was cursing a lot, and that wasn't the Kyle I knew. He was the good Canadian kid, all politeness and respect, and cursing as punctuation was not part of our vocabulary. "I sit there, and she rationalizes with me, then I leave the office and feel good, and there are no shadows. But then night happens, I fall asleep and they're back." He shifted where he sat and winced. I needed to look at his shoulder, but instinctively, I knew he needed to just sit and *be*.

"I picked up a can of shaving foam," I began because this was my job—I was the one who always lightened the tone, took down the crazy fear, and grounded him. At least it had been my job before he left. "I heard you yell, and I picked up shaving foam." I shook my head, embarrassed. "I don't know what I was going to do with it if there was a moose in the bathroom. Can you imagine?"

Silence. I forged ahead.

"I face off against twelve hundred pounds of outraged moose in my shower and spray it with shaving foam to get it to back off. It would have like a nose full of the stuff because hell, it's nearly empty. As if I really thought that a snout full of foam would actually mean a moose would leave my shower and trot out the front door with a wave."

He huffed a laugh, and I knew I'd hooked him.

"Only that was part one of my plan because if the shaving foam didn't persuade him to leave, you know what I would have done next?" I paused long enough to force him to respond.

"No, what?" He lifted his gaze to me, and his eyes were red from tears, but there was a soft quirk to his lips as if a smile was just sitting there waiting to happen.

"I would have gone for the mouthwash."

"The mouthwash?" This time his lips turned into a smile, and the fear in his expression faded a little.

"Moose don't like mouthwash. I mean, have you ever stood close to one? They love the unique scent of their breath which is eau-de-roadkill, and the thought of having minty freshness would be the last straw."

He snorted a soft laugh. I was winning against the shadows.

"So, I'd splash mouthwash at myself, and he would back away in horror and scamper out of the bathroom. I'd then open my front door and let him out, all the while shaking the mouthwash menacingly. Christian one, moose zero."

"How can you shake mouthwash menacingly?"

I painted an expression of horror on my face. "A ninja never shares his secrets to moose removal."

"The ninja code," he quipped, and abruptly we weren't twenty-five-year-old men in a cabin in the middle of a snowstorm. We were back to being kids, piling up wood for his mom and dad, and practicing our ninja moves so that the next time the shadows visited him, he would be able to fight them. It became our best friend's code, a pact between ten-year-olds who believed that channeling Chuck Norris was the only way to conquer all enemies. The ninja code was just another word for believing that we could defeat anything.

He shifted again, and this time he leaned against me, his forehead against my chest, his breath leaving him in one final sigh of fear.

"Fuck," he said with clear intent. "Fuck, shit, balls, fuck."

I couldn't resist the temptation of carding my hand through his hair. Yes, he'd gone to Boston, yes, he'd ghosted me, but here in this cabin, he was still the man I would always love, the one who held my heart in his hands. I should have fought more, should have camped outside the arena, but he hadn't wanted me there, and I'd listened to him.

Why did I listen to him?

His hair was still damp from the shower, and the ends were kinking a little. I rubbed the soft strands with my fingers, separating them, knowing that without product his black hair would curl if it was too long. He smelled of my shower gel, his breath minty, the weight of him against my chest was so familiar that I was desperate to tilt his chin and kiss away all the fears.

So desperate.

I cleared my throat, and he startled, then moved away from me.

"Sorry. I'm such a loser," he muttered to himself angrily.

"Yeah, well, if you don't practice the ninja code on a daily basis, that's what happens. Loser."

I flicked his forehead, and he winced, but at least he was smiling—even if he was clutching that damn stick.

"Right, stay there, I'll get the med kit and we'll fix your shoulder. Do you have painkillers in your bag?"

"Vicodin, but I don't want to use them too much—it's too easy to mask pain and not know what your body is actually doing."

"Did your doctor prescribe them?"

"Yep."

"Then you take them… he's not giving you meds for shits and giggles."

"I've seen addiction—"

I flicked him again to stop him from continuing to talk because the last thing that Kyle had was an addictive personality. Well, apart from sleeping with his hockey stick, but that wasn't an addiction, that was grounding him. There again, what did I know about Kyle and his personality anymore? Disgruntled and pissed at myself, I focused on pulling over my med kit and his backpack, handing them to him as I sorted through my kit for what I needed. I laid everything out on the table in front of the sofa on a sterile mat. Meanwhile, he was rummaging through his Rebels duffel, and then with a frown, he upended everything on the sofa next to him. Out came underwear, Rebels T-shirts, sweats, but not much else.

"Is that what you were going to wear every day?"

"It's comfortable," he defended.

I couldn't help but snort a laugh. "You were going to come down on Christmas Day dressed in sweats and a T-shirt? You realize Miriam would lose her mind over that given how seriously she takes the one dinner a year that is fancy?"

"There's a suit in the car," he said. "Other clothes, not much, but enough."

"So, you crashed the car, and you rescue this emergency duffel and your parents' gifts, but you leave what is probably some Hugo Boss suit in the cold icy coffin of your car?"

He blanched, and I wished I'd used any word except coffin, but it didn't faze him after that.

"It's actually Armani," he said and twisted a smile at me. "Blue."

He held up a familiar box with triumph. "Aha!" he said and then passed it to me. I had to break the seal, which didn't bode well for his pain management.

"Have you actually been taking these?"

"Not really—"

I placed them on the table. He needed some food in him before he took any, but the pain he had to be in must be a world of hurt I hadn't ever experienced. I pulled the robe off his shoulder and winced at the start of bruising across his chest from the accident, then felt sick when I saw the stitches in his shoulder.

"I saw them take you off the ice," I admitted.

"You did?" He sounded so surprised, as if his going off to Boston meant that I wasn't following his career anymore. Wasn't I the one who went to every game with him here, played alongside him until it became obvious I would never be more than an average skater and he was destined for big things? I might not want to watch him play when I was with his dad for our game nights, but I watched highlights and any game the local TV showed highlights from.

"Not live, but they showed it on the news, y'know, local NHL star, blah, blah. I couldn't believe the way Novikov barreled into you." I was so damn defensive I could have driven to Arizona and had strong words with the Raptors Captain, even if it was obviously just an accident

"It wasn't deliberate—no one meant anything by it," he reassured, and I wondered if my emotions were plain on my face.

"Yeah well, whatever." And there went my ability to form words in a sentence. I concentrated on the wound site and used what I had in the bag to close the few stitches that had come loose. The blood was mostly dry. He'd probably knocked his shoulder in the shower or in his mad dash to escape an unseen demon, but it had only seeped a little, so I cleaned it and covered it. "I assume the damage is internal as well."

He sighed. I know there was all this secrecy about injury. After all, if he went back with a shoulder that was maybe not a hundred percent and the other team got wind of where he hurt, then he was vulnerable. Still, this was me and I was up here in Manitoba, and I wasn't saying a damn thing to anyone.

"Yeah."

I pulled back, examined my work with a critical eye, wishing I had more than the basic emergency medicine skills, and then pulled the robe back up and over it.

"Okay then, food, and meds, and then rest." I used my best no-nonsense tone, but he clasped my hand and held it firm.

"Thank you," he said with feeling. "Just… thank you."

SEVEN

Christian

I GENTLY UNPEELED MY FINGERS FROM KYLE'S AND PATTED him on his good shoulder, and when he flinched, I knew I'd made things one-hundred-percent awkward. I should be able to take his thanks, and the touch of his hand on mine, and not feel my heart crack, right? We'd been dangerously close to smiling at each other over shared memories, and that was opening myself up for too much hurt.

"It's my job," I dismissed his thanks and then turned to find something else to do that didn't involve looking at Kyle.

We ate the food, and an hour passed where I did everything I could to not be anywhere near Kyle, but when I finally checked on him, he'd slumped sideways and was asleep. He looked so much like the old Kyle when he slept. I'd stared so many times at him sleeping in the past—waiting for him to wake with night terrors—that I knew his face well. He was certainly older, but he hadn't changed much, and I expected more given it had been so long since we'd last seen each other face-to-face.

Sometimes the camera would stop on his face in net, but there was very little I could make out behind his mask apart from his piercing gaze. The team photo told me nothing, apart from the fact that I could see the fear in his eyes even when he was smiling. Sometimes he was in the slo-mo shots of the players getting off the team bus at other venues, but after watching one of those, I refused to let myself look again.

I should have gone with him.

My inner voice was wrong—he didn't want me to go. He wanted to learn a new way of living where the terrors inside his brain didn't chase him every day, but had that worked? What had finally sent him back to us… was it just the injury? What happened in the bathroom freaked me out. I might have joked about the ninja code, but shit, there had been real fear in his shout, and I wondered if the ghosts from here had simply followed him to Boston.

Maybe they rode him every second and never left him alone.

I could have protected him from them. I should have gone with him.

I didn't have internet here, but what I wouldn't give to be able to scroll through photos of him in Boston and see if the fear was in each one. I'd know if it was by the way he slouched a certain way, or if the smile he was using didn't reach his eyes. He murmured in his sleep, but it was a mumble of nothing. I picked up the patterned blanket and laid it over him, tucking in the edges so he wouldn't get chilled. That was the host in me looking out for a guest, not the former lover in me that knew he got cold in bed and needed extra covers.

And then I stared at him. I watched his breathing, learning each inch of his face again, from his lashes to every faint mark, even the tiny scar from the great tree swing incident when we were eight. In my defense, I hadn't meant to shove him as hard as I did, but I slipped—that was my excuse, and I was sticking to it. He'd flown out over the lake and whooped so hard, on the high of fighting gravity, that he didn't even care when he hit the tree on the way back in. Of course, that was another time when we had a stern talking to from respective parents, but you bet we did it again. Only we learned how not to hit the tree on landing.

I decided that memories were a shit thing to focus on, so I checked in with a couple of people in town and called up Search and Rescue. No one needed my help in town, no one was out wandering about in the snow. It seemed like the only one out there was Kyle, and I'd kind of rescued him already. Loosely. With nothing else to do, I picked up a book and curled up at the other end of the sofa, away from Kyle.

The book wasn't holding my attention, at least not enough to stop me from staring at Kyle. I needed to work my way through my feelings before he woke up—get some defenses in place so I didn't buckle under the weight of all the emotions inside me.

He left. That was point one. The day he'd driven away from Eagle Ridge, I'd waved him off as if he was going to the next town for groceries. We'd woken that morning in each other's arms, but it had been okay for him to go. After all, he was coming back when he could, and I was going to visit him in Boston as soon as I wasn't needed here. No one else could run the store. No one else had my skills and understanding of the town to keep everyone safe, but I planned on heading down about six weeks after he left. Then there was the fact he was up in Canada again for various games, *and* there was Christmas, which he'd promised to come back for.

I couldn't make it to Boston. Things had happened at the store, in town, with my parents, with *life*, and he was focusing on being a rookie in an original six team. We had busy, tiring lives, and anyway, that was what FaceTime was made for. For the times we did connect, we made the most of it… enthusiastic phone sex was a thing.

Until it wasn't.

I hated that I'd let things slide. I wanted to sit next to him now and hold him and tell him I was sorry and that I loved him, and I wished I'd ignored his shit and forced myself into his new life. I hadn't done any of those things and instead I'd let him get away with hiding himself away.

Every time I asked him if the dreams had chased him to Boston, he'd change the subject, laugh it off as if the nightmares and fear were nothing. He blamed his parents, he blamed town, he said it was his old life that scared him. With hindsight, I'm convinced it was self-preservation—

convincing himself that he was okay in Boston. He wanted to distance himself from Eagle Ridge, and slowly, I realized he wanted to forget me. It wasn't anything obvious at first—missed calls, exhaustion, work on both our sides, an important game for him, a vital rescue for me —life got in the way for both of us, and somehow all the little things had become more.

Then he must have realized the best way to deal with his demons was to ghost me.

Or maybe I ghosted him.

Hell, we probably ghosted each other, if I'm being honest with myself. I hated that he didn't need me after needing me for so much of our lives. I resented that he was finally happy and didn't want me. All that poison balled up inside me, and I went through the stages of grief—loss and pain became acceptance, and I consigned him to the past. I hoped I could avoid him completely, given I was out in the woods. However, I never expected him to land at my door…

Nature had a way of wrecking even the best laid plans.

"Are you staring?" he mumbled, and I startled so bad I dropped my book.

"No," I lied. "I was lost in thought."

"Were your thoughts about me?"

I huffed a laugh. "Nope, you're not that important, Lourenco."

"Says you," he said with an added grimace as he struggled to sit up. "Can I get some…" His tongue darted out to wet his lips. "… I feel wooly," he muttered.

I fetched him water, and he took a few healthy swallows. "Better?"

"I hate meds," he added as if I hadn't understood what he meant by wooly. Had he slipped in the big city and chosen a different way of dealing with his fears?

"You said you'd seen addiction?" I asked with caution.

"You play the game long enough that it sometimes takes a guy swallowing pills just to drag themselves out on the ice."

"Is that you?"

His eyes widened. "Fuck no. It's like you don't know me at all." He added the last as a joke, but it was true—I didn't know him anymore, not really. Then he blinked at me, and I could see the gears working in his head and he gave a little shrug, with an added wince. "Nah, I'd retire before I couldn't play without pain."

"Have they given you a long-term prognosis for the shoulder?"

"It's all good," he said immediately, but I could tell he was lying. They might have said he'd heal, but I sensed he was worried. "Well, good until I drove into a tree. And maybe not quite as good as I thought. I've seen other goalies get railroaded, and some of them didn't come back."

"You'll be back," I said with fierce determination. Kyle was strong and stubborn, and fought demons far worse than an opposing team crashing his net.

He sent me a wry look. "You always were in my corner."

I didn't know what he meant by that, but a spark of warmth settled in my chest. I needed to hear that he knew I'd always have his back, whatever. The glance turned to something different, a faltering smile, and that spark began to grow. I wasn't ready for Kyle to drive back into my life and for me to lower all my barriers at just one smile.

"Want to play Monopoly?" I blurted when I couldn't think of anything else.

"Sure?" The agreement was more of a question, but his smile dimmed a little. Was he expecting us to have a heartfelt chat about life when he was dopey on Vicodin and I was hiding my love for him in a tiny dark part of my heart? *Nope. Not happening.*

I went to the bedroom and dragged down a battered box of Monopoly, brushing off the dust and straightening one corner that was torn and needed to be fixed. We'd played this game so many times, handed down to us from his dad, and maybe playing this wasn't the best way to combat memories.

"Did you ever find the hat?" he asked as I laid the box on the small kitchen table. The hat was lost to the past, somewhere between one game and the next it had vanished, and it had been my favorite playing piece—his was the car. I'd searched everywhere for it, but I never did find it, and the fact he recalled that single memory made my avoiding-emotion plan skew off-course.

"Nah, I still use the iron."

"I still think it was Yoda who ate it."

Shit, another memory we shared—childhood pets.

Yoda, the Lourenco family dog, cunning, always hungry, and the softest cuddler I'd ever met. The day we lost Yoda was one of the saddest of my childhood. I can remember the ceremony that Kyle and I had when we buried him. Full of kind words about our adventures—we'd been so grown up at ten—as Dad covered him with dirt. I recall backing away from the ceremony at that moment, crying, and running into the woods, Kyle on my heels. I missed Yoda.

"Maybe," I concentrated on dishing out cash.

"Do you remember the day that Yoda—"

"So, you're the car," I interrupted and slid the piece over to the start then held out the dice. "You go first."

He cradled my hand with the dice in the palm and squeezed. "Are you okay?" I focused on him, and he stared back with open affection in his expression. Sitting diagonally to him like this, all I needed to do was lean in a little and I could kiss him. Kissing him would stop the questions, but it wouldn't keep all the memories locked away in my head where they belonged. I wanted him back in my life so badly, but I was supposed to be angry with him.

I tugged my hand away. "Yep. Let's play."

We played in silence for the first few times around the board, and slowly, the memories began trickling into my thoughts. Not just Yoda but other pets, other times we'd been together, and when Kyle landed on Go To Jail, I crowed at his failure just as I would have before.

Then he snorted a laugh and shoved at my arm. "You

just watch me throw a double six, and I'll be out and buying Park Place in one go," he bragged.

That wasn't how it happened, but the game was easier from then on. With the storm raging outside, we slipped into playing this old game, and the silence was comfortable. He called me an asshole when he landed on my hotel and nearly bankrupted himself. I cursed at him when the hotel on Park Place that he'd built meant I was wiped out. He won, and he even did a small victory dance in his chair. The goofball.

The beautiful, sexy, vulnerable goofball.

We'd killed a few hours with the game, and it was time for more Vicodin. I noticed that, this time, he didn't argue at all, lines of strain around his mouth, and his eyes heavy with exhaustion. It was easy to forget that he'd crashed a car and that he'd already been injured.

"I finally got a tattoo," he announced when we settled back on the sofa. He yawned widely as I searched for a reason why he'd announced that out of the blue. We'd always talked about getting tattoos together one day, matching ones of a maple leaf, or something to do with one of our adventures, but I'd never had one done. It was supposed to be something we did together, not some random thing to do on our own.

"I saw."

He looked confused but then appeared to put two and two together. "When you looked at my shoulder. Yeah. Do you like it?"

"It's…" *sexy, hot, stunning*, "good." *Good? Lame, Christian, lame*.

"Did you read it?" He sounded so hopeful, and I didn't want to admit I'd taken in every cursive mark. The words didn't make sense, but they talked about ghosts, and I imagined it was something from his mom's heritage.

"Not really," I lied.

"Oh." He paused. "Did you ever get a tattoo?"

"We promised we'd get one together, so no, I haven't." Why did I do that? Why did I push the knife deeper? I'm a fucking idiot. I needed to get off this subject and talk about something else, maybe another memory that didn't hurt so much. Then I could stop focusing on wanting to kiss him, or hurt him, or touch him. I wanted to bury my hands in his hair, make sure he was real and sitting next to me. I wanted to have him in my arms, and…

… I just wanted to touch him.

EIGHT

Kyle

I'D NEVER FELT MORE FOOLISH IN MY LIFE BRINGING UP
the fact I had a tattoo now, and this from a man who had
once streaked out into the frigid waters of Hudson Bay on
a dare. Yes, it had been Christian who'd dared me. We'd
been thirteen and bulletproof, or so we'd thought. I nearly
went into shock and Christian, heroic dumbass that he is,
raced out to save me. I'd not really been drowning... I'd
just been terrified when my balls receded into my body.
Still, word got back to our parents—obviously—as nothing
stays secret for long in Eagle Ridge. We'd both been
grounded, and Christian had discovered his calling for
rescue work. Well, that incident and the time we rescued
Mr. Smith's cat Piddles from a tree. We'd each gotten a
toonie as a reward when Piddles was reunited with old Mr.
Smith. Mom had told me he was still tottering around in a
rundown cabin about a half mile or so up the road from
Christian. Mom also told me that Christian kept a good eye

on Mr. Smith. Piddles was long gone—obviously—but he had a new cat whose name escaped me.

Seemed Christian was good at taking care of people. Even the stupid ones like me. Thinking about my freak-out made my cheeks hot. I'd not had a slip that bad in years. Ever since the last time I'd come home. The dreams had ramped up, but I'd not seen imaginary shapes skulking around in a blizzard. As much as I loved my hometown and the people who lived here, I couldn't wait to put some distance between me and Eagle Ridge. The place was crawling with shadow people that only I could see and feel. It was like living in some B-grade horror flick.

Hence the tattoo. It was an interpretation of a traditional Inuit song my mother used to sing when I was caught up in the night terrors. It told the story of a spear shaman who acted as protector to his tribe by singing to the polar bear, the fox, and the wolf. With the blessings of all the creatures from the ptarmigan to the beluga whale, he kept his people safe. Once I was away from Christian, I needed that protection, and so. had the song inked into my back. Had it helped? Not as much as I would have liked.

TWO DAYS PASSED WHERE WE EDGED AROUND EACH OTHER, cautious of what to say, trapped in the cabin, both unsure. Sometimes we smiled, sometimes there was a glimpse of our old friendship, but mostly we were a mess of nothing at all. I slept a lot of it, but in my lucid moments I recalled all those moments when Christian saved me. Not just from the icy lake, but from all the nightmares that kept me a prisoner. I never stopped loving him, I'd simply escaped my terrors in this town and never come back.

The only problem was that I'd taken my terrors with me.

Sometimes he was angry, made a comment about me deserting him, and then just as quickly biting his tongue. Other times he would fondly recall something we'd done together, and my heart hurt so badly I thought it might crack.

Then, this morning, I'd woken to find him behind me on the bed, cradling me, and I pretended to sleep until he woke and realized where he was. He left the room in a hurry and didn't look back, but I know he must have come in to take away a nightmare. I'd felt him there, and for the first time in so many years, I'd woken up with peace in my head instead of fear.

Then, after breakfast, he'd looked so confused as we cleared away dishes, and tidied the kitchen, throwing me glances that made my stupid damaged heart leap.

"… jumped off the Empire State building and did a hero landing."

My attention flew to Christian seated beside me on the sofa. "Iron Man?"

"No, me."

I rubbed my eyes with my right hand. My left was dangling out of the sling. "When did you join the Avengers?"

"I didn't, idiot. I was telling you about Mr. Smith's new cat, Delilah, then I asked if you remembered Piddles. What an unfortunate name for a cat. Kind of prophetic, too, as he started piddling on the floor when he got old. You never answered. Are you okay?"

"Oh yeah, I'm fine. I think the Vicodin is kicking in. It makes me fuzzy-headed."

I want to kiss you. I want to stop you feeling confused.

"You've always been fuzzy-headed," he joked, his hand going to my hair to ruffle it playfully. That old, familiar action had a different effect on me than it had when we were ten. Back then, I'd wrestle him to the floor and make him eat a crayon or a dirt clomp. This evening, with the winds roaring and sleet peppering the windows, his fingers on my scalp made me yearn for more touching. Of any kind. Instinctually, I tipped my head up like a cat seeking a better scratch, my eyes falling closed. There was this long moment where his fingertips just rested on my head. Then, slowly, they began to gently massage my scalp. I may have purred just like good old Piddles. Or Delilah. Pick a cat.

"What are we doing here, Kyle?" I don't think it was a real question, and he sighed. "I thought this was…" I wanted him to finish the sentence, but he didn't. Instead, he changed the subject. "Did you want to talk to your parents?"

"They know I'm here; I don't feel right yet. My head is so…" I yawned and sighed heavily. I didn't want to have to answer all the questions, but I had spoken briefly to them as soon as I could, promised I'd stay at the cabin, and told them I was okay. I owed them a longer chat, because I didn't know how many days I'd be in the cabin with Christian. Tomorrow for sure.

"Okay, so let's watch another movie," he said in a voice smoky as an Easter ham. I mumbled something about nothing scary. He chuckled. My eyes opened slightly. Sadly, his hand then left my head to fumble with the remote. I peeked to the side. He was intent on what he was doing, his brow furrowed, as he poked around in his DVR for movies. The small satellite dish on the roof was unable to pick up a signal. It was probably packed with snow and ice, so we'd have to make do with what was sitting in his list.

"How about *The Emperor's New Groove*?"

My heavy lids flew up at the mention of that movie. "You seriously have that recorded?"

"Sure. Any time I have a bad day, I come home and watch it. Nothing makes me laugh harder than Kronk."

"Same here. And Yzma "

"Man, we loved that movie, didn't we?" Christian's face was illuminated by the TV, and seeing his smile made my heart skip several beats. Why had I not pressed him harder to come to Boston with me? Why had I let him slip through my fingers? No man would ever be what Christian was to me. My heart had always belonged to him, and it always would. "You cool with this?" he asked, then looked my way, the lighthearted expression slipping when our eyes locked. "Kyle…"

I wasn't sure which of us leaned in first. Maybe it was me, maybe it was Christian. Didn't matter. As soon as our lips met, nothing else in the world mattered. Not the blizzard, the shadow men, the years of separation. When my mouth moved over his—guess I was the instigator, which was different for a goalie, but I'd roll with it—my world slipped back onto its axis. Most people would be the opposite of that, but not me. Nope. The feel of his lips pressed to mine righted so many wrongs in my life. I moved to the side to try to get my right hand onto the nape of his neck. He pulled back, his emerald eyes wide.

"Kyle, we really shouldn't be doing this. You're on drugs, and I'm…" He stumbled verbally, and I took that opportunity to steal another kiss. He sighed into my mouth, and all was lost. Our tongues tangled. The world outside of this cabin—this sofa—ceased to exist. I moved into him, sliding to the side, my left arm pinned between us in that stupid sling.

"Kyle," he whispered when I moved to straddle him. "Your arm."

"My heart," I whispered against his lips, pushing back the pain and loving when his hands settled on my hips, guiding me down onto him gently.

"Christian," I replied breathlessly, my free hand sliding into the short, thick, dark mass of his hair as I moved against him. He arched up, his ass leaving the sofa, and we were done. Not that I had any intentions of leaving his lap any time soon, but that one movement sealed it. I lowered my mouth back to his and let myself get lost in him. The kisses got hotter, sloppier, and more desperate. He cupped my ass, a thick guttural sound erupting out of somewhere deep within him and I gasped into his mouth and came. Just like that. As if I were sixteen and this was our first time together.

My cock kicked, I moaned against his cheek, and my body shuddered.

"Yes, Kyle, come for me," he growled as I pumped a heavy load into my underwear. His mouth claimed mine in a crushing kiss as he jerked and spasmed under me, his orgasm ripping through him. My fingers raked his scalp, and I bit down on his neck, right where it joined his shoulder, as hard as I could. He yelped in pain/pleasure just as I remembered. I licked into his mouth as he twitched and massaged my ass. When the world began to come back into view, I let my head fall to his shoulder and not even the pain stopped me from kissing the mark I'd left on his pale skin. Then I worked my way back to his mouth. His lips were pink, wet, and puffy. I stole several small kisses, tender little things that he sighed into, the contented sound a balm to my soul.

"So that just happened," he said a few minutes later. I rocked into him again. He held me in place, our cocks flaccid now. "I'm not sure it should—"

I kissed him into silence, then slithered carefully off to the side, my fingers still laced into his hair. I pulled him downward, easing my arm out of the way, spread my legs for him. He eased between my thighs as if he were crafted by Mom's Inuit Gods to be there and rested gently without putting his weight fully on me. I let my eyes drift shut as he nuzzled at my throat, whispering soft things as lovers do. My right hand remained fisted in his hair until I drifted off, safe and secure, his body serving as the best blanket ever created. Not one dream disturbed me. As it had always been, Christian was who kept the unseen shadows at bay.

When I came awake sometime later, the cabin was dark, the TV off, and my burly blanket of a man was gone. His grandmother's quilt covered me. I eased myself up, wincing at the pull of the new stitches in my shoulder. The cabin was quiet save for the pop and hiss of green pine logs in the fireplace. Confused and sleepy, I slid my hand into my pocket to find my phone to check the time. My underwear was sticking to the fine hairs of my lower belly. I wiggled a bit to try to free the cotton from the dried spunk, but was unsuccessful. Gross. Easing my phone free from my pocket, I took note of the silence. The wind had tapered off by the sounds. It was still as dark as a polar bear's butthole, as Pops would say, but maybe we'd ridden out the worst of it.

Yawning, I checked the time. Six minutes after seven. And still dark. Ugh, winter nights on the bay seemed eternal. Course it could be worse. We could be living in Norway where they had something like twenty-four hours of darkness. Or was that light? I always got confused. Whatever it was, nights here dragged on forever in the winter. I pushed to my feet and pattered to the front door. Flicking on the porch light, I gasped at the amount of snow that had piled up outside. Easily three or more feet, much of it windswept leaving a huge mound in front of the door that would require shoveling. I scowled down at my slinged arm, then flipped off the porch light, leaving the snow to set until Christian woke up. What else could I do? I was useless. Mad at myself for being so frigging slow, I dug into my duffel for some clean clothes. A shower was a must. I crept past Christian's open door. The urge to crawl into bed with him and take his cock into my mouth was strong, but I opted to be mature. Just for once. He'd been into what had happened on the sofa, obviously, or at least physically he was into it. Afterward, he'd expressed something much like regret, or so it had sounded to my ears. Until we could talk about that hot frottage session, I should keep my hands—and mouth—to myself.

The bathroom was chilly, but quickly warmed. I peeled off my clothes and sling, easing my stiff arm down, then out to the side. My shoulder was bruised, the flesh tender, and it ached, but overall, I could deal with the pain. Maybe if I'd not been loopy on pain meds, I'd not have kissed Christian. Maybe I would have too. There was no denying the gravitational pull he had on me. I was nothing more than a tiny moon spinning around his celestial body, unable to break free even if I had wanted to, which I didn't.

After my shower, I pulled on my around-the-house clothes and slipped into the kitchen. The washer sat in a small alcove, so while I made coffee, I dumped my dirty laundry into the stacked washer/dryer combo and tossed in some soap. My cup was full when I returned to the kitchen. I rustled around in the fridge, found some milk, sniffed it, and then poured a dollop into my coffee.

"You make coffee real loud," Christian mumbled as he loped into the kitchen, his hair a mess, his face thick with dark brown stubble, and his old tee still twisted around his wide shoulders. He was beautiful. I found it hard to speak, his beauty moved me so. I didn't know what to say or do. It was such an awkward moment. What did you say to the man that you had major unrequited love for when you rode his stiff prick like a mangy mutt?

"I'm sorry," tumbled out of me. He gave me a confused look then made a beeline to the Keurig.

"For what?" He tried to cram a new pod in when the old one was still in place. "Dumbass," he chided himself, then whipped my used pod into the sink and dropped a new one in its place.

"For taking advantage of you last night."

His sleepy green gaze flew from the coffee maker to me. His brows knitted. "You didn't take advantage of me. How could you have? You're injured, and I'm bigger than you."

"Heavier maybe, but I'm taller." I felt it was important to point out. Why? No damn clue. "I think I was feeling less in control of myself. The pain meds probably, but not all of it. Maybe they just made me feel freer to express my lust for you, but—"

He held up a hand roughed from work. I stood there

staring at the swirls of his finger pads, suddenly yearning to touch my lips to each fingertip.

"Okay, let's get this cleared up. You did *not* force me into anything. I wanted to kiss you, Kyle. I wanted to do a lot more than that."

"Tell me," I asked in a shallow whisper. His eyes grew hot.

"I wanted to take you to my bed, lay you down, and taste every inch of you. I wanted to familiarize myself with the taste of your cock, the weight of your balls, the snug heat of your tight ass."

"Oh fuck," I croaked as he adjusted the thick ridge of his dick through his jogging pants.

"Yeah, oh fuck." His voice was gruff and deep. I set my mug on the counter. "So, you can stop with the whole 'you made me do something that I didn't want to do' act. I wanted what happened to happen just as much as you did. No one has ever made me feel as you do, Kyle, and I got caught up in the smell of your skin and the nostalgia of you, but I'm not sure that wistfulness is a good enough reason to rekindle what we had."

My heart cracked inside my chest, but I nodded. He was right. We couldn't just fall into bed because of some teenaged fling. Sure, he still cradled my heart in his strong, capable hands, but I was a mess. Probably it would be a kindness for me to let him go. What do they say about if you love something you should turn it loose?

"Of course, you're right. I just… coming home and then the wreck. Finding you and having you so close… it was just dumb. I won't kiss you again. You deserve someone who's not scared of his own hometown and can give you what you want."

His expression changed immediately, and he looked kind of stormy. "How do you know what I want? You ran out on me, your folks, and this whole damn town! After all we did for you. We all supported you, cheered at all your games, and as soon as you could, you fucking left!"

Wow, ouch, okay. That was all justified for sure, yet it still rankled. "I had to leave. I asked you to come with me. We could have made a life in Boston, a good one!"

"What would I have done in Boston, huh? My life is here—people need me here."

"You thrive on being that guy who everyone depends on, but once you leave this little pond, you're just a scared little cod!"

He blinked at me, and all the anger vanished. "A cod. Did you just call me a cod?"

"Yeah, I did. A fish-faced cod." He started to chuckle. That made me good and mad. "You smell like one too!"

"Oh, holy shit. What are we, eight?" Then he broke up. I stood there seething, vulnerable, and terrified of losing him forever, and he was howling in mirth. Tears streaming down his face, holding his stomach, roaring in laughter. "Fish… face!" I sniggered a bit. Fuck, that *was* kind of childish. "You always were the worst chirper."

"I know." I rubbed at the back of my neck as I chuckled softly.

"You drive me insane, Kyle. I swear I never know what

the hell is up or down when you're around." His green eyes were wet with unshed tears, his lips smiling. I adored that smile.

"You don't smell like cod."

"Yeah, I know."

"Maybe char or whitefish, but not cod."

"Asshole." He wiped at his eyes with the hem of his shirt, giving me a nice peek at his abs. Mm, they were firm and furry. I wanted to rub my face on his belly. "What are we going to do here, Kyle?"

"Maybe have breakfast and talk?"

NINE

Christian

Kyle evidently wasn't very good at talking this morning.

Instead, he made a whole song and dance on his enthusiasm about the pancakes being soft fluffy discs of perfection, his words not mine. Then he commented at length on the syrup that formed a river around them and munched his way through a pile of crispy bacon, which rated its own dissertation. The one thing he *didn't* talk about was us. I couldn't believe he'd suggested I'd been too scared to leave town because I was a big man here. I was anything but.

I was part of the fabric of this town, the person who would help anyone, the one that put his life at risk to keep others safe. Nearly dying when I was rescuing the kids had shaken me, but it was my job, and I was damn good at it. And the store was my job—I kept the town ticking over. People relied on me. If I'd gone to Boston, I'd have been lost—maybe would have ended up losing my shit in a huge empty house. What kind of relationship was that to have?

"Breakfast of champions." Kyle pushed his plate away and patted his belly. "You know maybe this is the issue, not enough Canadian inside me." His eyes widened as he realized what he'd said, and then he smirked. "Get it?"

Of course, I got it, but if I reacted to that, then we'd fall into banter, and right now, I wanted at least a small bit of seriousness. I chose to ignore him and thought about the best way to get him to talk about the things that really mattered—like why he was still jumping at shadows from his childhood nightmares when he promised me that he'd get them fixed when he went away to play.

Him being at peace was half the reason I didn't argue about him heading south for hockey—the other half I put down to stupidity on my part.

"Tell me about Boston." That was a nice gentle start.

"It's a city on the East coast," he deadpanned, but I wasn't going to be led away from the core matter of what in hell's name was going on here.

"And you're seeing a counselor," I began, and he winced before heaving a sigh. Maybe he thought we wouldn't be talking about what was going on in his head, but hell, that was exactly what I wanted to cover. Well, that and the whole getting off with each other. He opened his hand and counted on his fingers.

"Team psych. Although to be fair, Bob is a goalie coach and comes at this from the perspective of the game. I don't tell him about the nightmares, he just puts my weird shit down to being a goalie and gives me a solid perspective on my game. I get away with being weird and he never even comments. Privately, I see Dr. Maynard every three weeks. He understands the night terrors happen, but given I have no idea why I have them, then we're at an impasse." He stopped counting his fingers.

"That's it?" I don't know what I was asking, but I expected him to have more support in Boston, not just two people he talked to on a regular basis.

"I handle it."

"Clearly," I huffed, and he winced at my tone. I immediately felt contrite, but the huff still stood because he obviously wasn't taking this seriously.

"What about friends? The team? Your new captain, Xander, is he supportive?"

"Of course."

"Of course, to what part of that?"

"Xander. He's a good captain, wants to make things right for everyone. Also, I have Austin, and somehow, he makes things better," he said in all seriousness, and my heart stopped.

"Austin."

"Rowe, one of Tennant's cousins, bit of a wunderkind, new to the team, he's—"

"I know who freaking Austin Rowe is, Kyle. This is Manitoba, not Mars." Hell, I was the one that wanted to play hockey on the team two towns over. He just followed me, then eclipsed my mediocre skills, so yeah, I might not watch Kyle when he's playing, but I know hockey, and you'd better believe I knew every stat of the Boston Rebels. Austin had his cousin's good looks, the same endearing smile, the hockey skills, and something that felt a lot like jealousy burned in my chest.

"We share an apartment, and we room together when we're on road trips. He's…" He waggled his fingers and then frowned. "Peace, I guess. He's understanding, never comments on my quirks, just always tries to help."

"Help how?" I know I sounded suspiciously like a mad man, but I had images of Austin Rowe hugging him as I did, or sleeping with him, or being the new person in his life that could quiet the nightmares. Were they lovers? Was this the moment I realize that any remaining flicker of hope was going to be snuffed out?

Then why would he kiss me?

Could I be any more dramatic right now? He left town. He moved on. It was just a kiss and rubbing off. I didn't stop him. But he's mine… I only had to kiss him again, and I knew that when he left, my heart would be shut to anyone else. I always said I was Kylesexual, and it was true. I hadn't had a relationship before him, and none since he left, because I was like a lobster, or a crab, or whichever crustacean mated for life. Kyle was imprinted on me and that was it as far as I was concerned. I'd once tried to date this perfectly normal guy from the city. One date and I'd realized my Kylesexuality was a fixed constant.

"When Austin first invited Robbie over, he saw me on the sofa, y'know, ear buds in, and he turned his back to me to talk to the guy. He probably thought I couldn't hear, but the playlist had ended, and I heard every word." He cleared his throat. "Austin very carefully explained I needed my space and sometimes I had dreams, but that it didn't matter. He was so in love with Robbie, yet he was defending me and warning him to keep out of my face. That's pretty cool, I think. He's a good friend."

"Wait. Rowe and this Robbie are a couple?" The relief that flooded me made me pause.

"Yep, cute as well. So young, but when you know, you know." He glanced at me, and his cheeks reddened. I should be grateful he had someone in his life that helped him with the fears, but selfishly I wanted…

What? What did I want? The kiss had been a passionate reminder that we'd gone from being best friends to being lovers a long time ago, and that even now, just one touch was enough to reconnect us if we let it.

"You said we should talk." He hesitated for a moment. "So, I guess we need to talk."

The wind was louder against the windows and the snow kicked up again, a cacophony of knocks and taps against the cabin, and even though he tried really hard not to, I caught Kyle's wince.

I'd held hope that sending him away would quell the constant fear that dogged him. Hell, when I'd let him go —sent him away—I did it hoping that, somehow, he'd find peace when he focused on his career and maybe even love in a new city. He didn't need me reminding him of all his insecurities and fears. Hell, I even thought he'd find friends who cared more than even I could, or make a new family for himself down there. Clearly, he'd made friends, Austin for one. I knew the team and the pundits called him Renco, and that he was the brick wall of the Boston Rebels. People cared for him, case in point Austin Rowe. But nothing had changed for the man I loved. He was still in a world of his own, which I bet most would put down to goalie eccentricity, but which I knew was deep-rooted in anxiety. The only time he was truly centered was when he was between the pipes in a game, so maybe his anxiety was easier to hide in Boston? I wish I knew for sure.

"Coffee first." I needed to make fresh coffee to give myself time to consider what I was going to say. I couldn't exactly turn around and tell him that the whole point of me letting him go without a fight had apparently meant nothing at all. If the dreams followed him, then he wasn't happier away from me. When I sat down, making sure to put distance between us, I still didn't have any idea what I wanted to say, and I stared into my mug and hoped that somehow the words would just happen.

"Why did you let me go?" Kyle interrupted my navel gazing.

I felt the words as if they were a physical blow. He knew why I hadn't stopped him—I told him that his talents were being wasted, that he needed to go. We'd had a rational conversation about long-distance relationships. After all, being apart had worked when he was away in Winnipeg, playing for the Walleyes in the minor leagues. Or at least we'd gotten used to it. Boston was farther than

Winnipeg, but I could travel to the nearest place with Internet, and we had love on our side.

He'd fallen for all my bullshit and left without looking back.

"You had so many more chances being away from here," I finally said. *Being away from me and escaping the weird ass nightmares.*

"I was alone."

"What did you want me to do? Follow you down to a city that didn't need me when I have a life here?"

"No. But you could have had a life with me."

"What about my family? Your family? The people who need me up here? The store?"

"We could have made it work," he said stubbornly.

"How exactly? One of us was going to be happy, the other one miserable, what kind of relationship is that?"

He was getting agitated, placing his coffee mug on the table, and leaning forward on his chair. "So, we both ended up miserable?"

"I'm doing okay, and fuck you, I'm happy, at least I was until you dumped yourself on my doorstep." Anger coiled inside me. He didn't have the right to come back into my life and tell me I wasn't happy. I had the store, I had friends, I looked after the town, I rescued people in trouble, I was respected, and I wasn't bothered about a relationship. Not everyone needed a partner to be happy, and until he'd turned up, I never even questioned my solitary living.

"Shit, sorry, I didn't mean anything—"

"Then don't freaking say it, asshole."

He dipped his head in acknowledgment. I knew he didn't hate Eagle Ridge. He loved his parents, and we'd had so many good years here until the shadows and his talent took him away.

"We were in love," he continued with determination. "I asked you to come with me because it was always you and me against the world."

"Your world, Kyle. Not mine."

"Christian, you're wrong, we—"

"You gave up on us," I blurted. "You stopped coming home, texting me back, then calling me, then that was it… you didn't want to make it work. I get something about this place terrifies you, or maybe even me, and I don't know if it's commitment or isolation or not seeing a future where I'm part of it, but you didn't want me to help you work through it, you didn't want this, and I don't understand. You didn't want me."

He bent at the waist, his elbows on his knees. He was the picture of hopeless misery, and he didn't move.

"It's not you that terrifies me," he choked out.

"I lost my lover and best friend," I added quietly. "Why did you give up on us?"

"Christian," he began, and I thought he was crying. I wish he'd look up at me, but unless I asked him, he wouldn't move. "I can't do this."

My heart broke. Four simple words. He'd decided the fate of whatever we had, and now we were stuck in a cabin, cut off from the world. We'd potentially have days of having to be near each other while I came to terms with losing Kyle all over again.

"I understand," I lied. "Let's just get through the few days here, and then you can go back to Boston."

"No, you don't get it. I can't go back on my own. I can't do this anymore. I tried, but it's gotten worse, and I can't run away from *it* when *it* follows me everywhere." He was agitated and, finally, he glanced up at me and released the grip on his hair. I'd never seen such bleakness in one person's expression. "Help me, Christian, it wants me." I moved quickly, going to my knees in front of him, and lacing my fingers with his. It didn't matter that my heart hurt when I knew I could calm him with my touch.

"What do you mean?" I asked gently, and he stared at me with wide eyes.

"I've seen it."

"I don't understand."

"It's real."

"Kyle—"

"I think it's watching me."

"What? In your dreams?"

"No, for real. I see reflections of something. I don't know what I'm seeing, but my head hurts."

"From the hit on you?"

"No, I mean before that, as if I have all this blackness setting inside me, and I feel cold." To underscore that, he shivered, and I rubbed his hands. "We were in this coffee shop, some of the guys and I, playing Dungeons and Dragons, and I was a... that's not important. One of the guys, Joachim, Loafy, he left, and I watched him go out the door, then Xander followed, because he's a good captain, and Loafy clearly has issues with… no that's not important either."

He shook my hands free and scrubbed at his eyes.

"Talk to me," I urged when he stared at me in silence.

"There was this person, in a dark coat, with the hood up, staring into the shop. I'd seen them before I think. Never face on like this, but in glimpses out of the corner of my eye, there one minute and then gone."

"An overzealous fan?"

"No, I know them. They're the ones with jerseys, or they want to shake my hand, or get an autograph. They are smiles and light, and they make everything right for a moment. This person was malevolent." He stopped talking.

"That's a big word for such a little hockey player," I teased, wanting him to smile, but instead he gripped my hands again.

"I mean it. I closed my eyes, and they were gone. I don't know if I was imagining it, but I'd reached my limit and I went outside. Walked straight past where Xander and Loafy were talking, and searched for the shadow because I needed to confront it."

I didn't want to tell him he sounded manic because this wasn't any different from some of what I'd seen before when he woke from nightmares. The shadows in his head chased him, and whether it was an overactive imagination, or he was genuinely seeing something, I knew the fear was real.

"Did you find anything?"

He shook his head. "Of course I didn't. But that wasn't why I told you."

"Okay, I'll bite."

"I told you because that night I picked up my phone and wanted to call you so bad because you're that part of me that is bravery and compassion, and I needed that."

"But you never called."

"Because I fucked up. I loved you and I left, and it was the stupidest thing I ever did." He cradled my face and kissed me, deeply, passionately, and then he pulled back. "I love you, Christian. I always will."

I couldn't be anything but honest. "I'll always love you, too."

He smiled, and it made his eyes shine. "Wanna go back to bed?" he asked, and I stood so fast that I nearly tripped back over the table.

"Hell yes."

TEN

Kyle

HAVING CHRISTIAN TAKE ME BY THE HAND AND LEAD ME
to his room—to his *bed*—was a dream coming true. I'd
dreamt of this for years, a reconciliation where we ended
up making love. Then the credits would roll, we'd kiss,
and then we'd sail into a setting sun as warm tropical
winds made the palm trees sway.

The reality was a little different. There were no
dancing fronds, no warm tropical breezes, and no sailboat
under our sandals. What we had was snow up to our asses,
brutal winds right off a frozen bay, and probably a polar
bear checking out Christian's trash cans.

No matter. The setting wasn't all that important, the
leading man was. Christian was what made this fantasy.
He paused in the living room, with his fingers meshed with
mine.

"You want to find your stick?"

The fact he asked me that made me love him even

more. I wasn't sure that was possible but there it was. Love. Growing by leaps and bounds just like the Grinch's heart.

I shook my head. "You'll keep me safe."

He appeared to be stunned, then concerned, then resolute. "That's a lot of pressure to put on someone, Kyle, but I'll do my best to shelter you from the unseen."

With his words still dancing in my ears, I took the lead, eager now to tumble into his warm, soft mattress and let him claim me as his once more. I pulled him after me, into his room—the air a little chillier in here as the woodstove was in the main room—without a worry that we'd be cold. I turned to face him. He released my hand then cupped my face between his warm, rough palms. My heart was racing, but in a good way, and I wet my lips. He made a soft, grumbly sound and led my mouth to his. Our tongues tangled. I found his hips, clutched them firmly, and angled his pelvis. Then I ground into him. He grunted when our cocks rubbed against each other. My grip grew firmer as the kiss deepened, and my thrusts increased.

"Slow down," he whispered when shudders raced over me. "We have all the time in the world."

"Sorry I just… I want you so bad." The confession caught him off-guard for some crazy reason. "Did you think I stopped wanting you?" I asked, moving my hands up his sides, catching the edges of his shirt as I went. "I never stopped wanting you." Hitching up his shirt to his chin, I bent to drop a kiss to his pectoral. Muscles twitched under my lips, the hair on his chest tickled. Letting my eyes drift shut, I rubbed my cheek against his chest, loving the soft rub, as well as the way his heart was thundering just as mine was. "I never stopped loving you." I pulled the shirt up over his head, then returned to nuzzling and tasting his skin.

"Same... God... it was the same for me." My skin heated up at his admission. I toyed with a pink nipple, flicking it hard then sucking on it until he took my chin in his hand and led my mouth back to his. "You need to give me a minute."

"You still like that." I sighed, then gave myself over to him to do with me as he pleased. I wanted him to come, but I didn't want him to come. I wanted to watch him come apart, and yet I didn't want this to end. Not ever.

"I like it when *you* do it, baby, only you." He made short work of my clothing, his hands shaking a bit, his actions jerky. When I was nude, he fell to his knees. Before his mouth was near my leaking cock, I was moaning loudly. "You're still so vocal. Fucking love it."

When he swallowed me down, I cried out, shoving my fingers into his hair, easing my hips forward. He sucked hard, then pulled off, giving the underside of my prick a wet swipe of his tongue before focusing on lapping at my cockhead. I whimpered and groaned, my balls tightening, as he worked me with hand and mouth. When I was almost at the end of my rope, he eased off, cupping my balls gently, then giving them a squeeze.

"Christian," I gasped, teetering on the edge.

"I know, Kyle. I know, baby." He rose then, slowly,

peppered kisses over my abs, chest, and chin before licking into my mouth. My fingers began frantically working at his zipper.

"Want to suck you," I huffed as the zipper lowered. "Want to swallow down your load."

"Christ, Kyle." He shoved his pants and underwear down to his thighs. Dropping to my knees with a thud that made me wince, I did the rest. I helped him finish disrobing, then buried my face in the thick thatch of curls at the base of his fat cock. "Shit, Kyle, I missed this so much. Seeing you down there, eyes filled with adoration looking up at me."

"I adore your cock." I tongued the slit, shuddering wantonly as the tang of his precum hit my tastebuds.

"Do you adore me?" His tone was tight, but playful.

"Meh, you're okay." I tried not to snigger. He chuckled, then ran his thumb along my cheekbone, then across my lower lip.

"I adore you." I blinked. He was so earnest it hurt my heart.

"I love you, too," I whispered gruffly before taking him into my mouth. His hips stuttered, his left hand still cradling my face, his thumb resting at the corner of my mouth. He'd always been into getting his fingers into my mouth or ass as his cock moved in and out.

He pressed his thumb in. I worked my tongue over it as well as his prick. His words became a little slurred as he began pumping with more vigor. I was ready for him to coat my throat, but he eased me off, then reached down to help me up, careful not to tug on my left arm, but only lift me with his hand under my chin. We fell into the bed as he kissed me, legs and arms knotted like fishing lines on a windy day. I couldn't touch or taste him enough. He licked hot wet paths all over me, lifting my right arm to taste the underside of my biceps, then nibbling along my ribs, always mindful of my left arm. His mouth moved over me, his lips skimming over the tattoo on my back.

"Please, please," I begged after what seemed an eternity spent with his gentle caresses and soft kisses. "Please love me again."

"I never stopped so it can't be again," he whispered beside my ear before moving to rummage in the nightstand drawer. My heart may have exploded from delight seeing him rip open a birthday card that had three condoms in it.

"Do you think these are okay?" He asked doubtfully. "I don't actually have a supply, what with the not dating thing. These were a joke present from…" he glanced up at me.

"Yes!" I exclaimed before he could talk himself out of it. "Just use one. I'm negative, I've only ever been with you, come on."

His eyes widened at that, and then he removed one from the package and rolled it over his beautifully curved cock. "Lift your leg up, yeah, that's gorgeous. God, Kyle, you are the most stunning man."

He bent down to kiss me then slid a pillow under my ass. I lay there like a wet noodle, breathing hotly, my dick slick, as he coated his fingers with lube, then slowly worked two into me. I hissed. He stopped. I wiggled my ass down a bit, lessening the pressure on my shoulder, and then clamped around his fingers.

"More, please, more," I said, my hand roaming up his belly as he began working me open. Eyes closed, left arm tucked into my side, right massaging his pec, my body softened. "Please... Christian... please?"

"Yes, baby, yes." He eased his fingers out, then tapped my slick hole with his cock. "You're so beautiful, Kyle, so perfect. Easy now." My eyes flew open when he pressed in. It had been years, and his prick was fat. "Breathe. Yes good. Breathe."

"Oh God; so good!" I yelped as he pushed past that ring of resistance. "More, all of it. Give me all. Make me come. Love me."

"Always, baby, always." He began to move his hips. A moan rolled out of me as he began stroking my prick in time with his thrusts. My balls drew up in mere moments. Then he moved up just a bit, off his knees, and pegged my prostate. There was no stopping the orgasm that barreled into me like a Russian winger crashing the net. Cum pulsed out of me, coating his fingers and striping my chest. A droplet hit my cheek. I writhed and whimpered, then tensed around him when I felt his cock kick. I opened my eyes to watch him tumble. The sight was breathtakingly erotic, and perhaps the most beautiful thing I had ever witnessed. His head fell forward, his neck muscles bulged, my name falling from his lips.

Warmth filled me and I wished we had skipped the condom.

"Shit, ah shit," Christian gasped, slipping out of me once he had some control of his legs, then falling to the bed like a fallen oak. "Oh shit…"

"Such a word wizard," I teased, my own vocabulary not that much better than his. He laughed into the pillow, then slung an arm over my chest. There we lay, sweaty and spent, coated with spunk, and purring like cats in a creamery.

I felt him kiss my arm. I smiled at the ceiling and slid my ass off the pillow, rolling on top of him. He grunted, but simply shimmied over, his head coming up, a smile playing at the corners of his mouth.

"Maybe we don't need condoms," he murmured, "I haven't… I mean I haven't been with anyone, and I'm negative and—"

"Then maybe we don't. You've not lost your touch," I told him. He moved to his side, the bed shaking a bit, and stared into my soul. "I'm sorry I—"

He put his mouth to mine. "No more apologies. We both fucked up. No one is any more to blame than the other. Let's just start over from right here and right now. Yeah?"

"Yeah." I nodded, then stole another kiss. Then another and then another. Christian eventually had to pry my lips from his so he could take care of the condom. We washed up, touching, tickling, whispering, and laughing, and the world was ours. Somehow, we'd make it work this time. I didn't know how yet, but we would. We had to.

We dressed comfortably and padded out to the kitchen for food. Sex always made me hungry.

"Can we warm up some stew?" I asked. He nodded, his expression caring and soft now. I made a move toward him to go into his arms and thank him for the stew and for still loving a fuck-up like me. When I lifted my foot, a loud thud hit the back door, and then over the slowing of the storm, growling. We both startled sharply, my eyes going wide, my heart rate leaping instantly.

"It's probably just a limb," he assured me, reaching out to stroke my cheek before padding softly past the washer spinning my clothes.

I fell in behind him, curiosity making me brave. If there was a shadow man on the back porch, I'd not be alone in facing him down. Christian would be there with me. Strong, brave, loving Christian.

Please don't let it be Taqriaqsuit.

When he threw open the back door, it pushed aside a good foot of snow. He gave it a firmer shove to clear more snow out of the way. Bitter cold air rushed into the small corridor. I moved closer to his back, terrified, yet eager to see if a monster lurked out there in the arctic dawn or if it was just a dead white birch branch. It was neither.

A lone bloody boot lay on the back porch.

The doorway seemed to shift, rocking sideways, as a loud humming like a swarm of locusts overtook me.

The snow outside turned dark, blackish, and narrowed

into a small square. Hot, so hot, and tight. My knees were under my chin, my nose plugged, my face damp, my feet cold and bare. Someone walked past me on the right, humming a song that was scary... a grown-up with big boots covered with blood. Fresh, sticky, bright red blood. Arterial blood.

Then the present came crashing back, all white and silent. I listed left, clawing at Christian before I hit the floor like a fallen tree.

ELEVEN

Christian

TOO MANY THINGS HAPPENED AT ONCE. A SQUALL OF WIND and snow hit me dead on and yanked the door back out of my hold, peppering my skin with icy shards. There was blood on my porch in the only part of it not buried in snow, under the shelter of a shelf and signs of a scrap between wild animals. Then there was Kyle, who'd crumbled at my side and slumped to the floor as if his strings had been cut. I prioritized because whatever animals dumped a blood and bite covered boot on my porch could well be out there still, and the last thing we needed was for us to be in a battle to the death with an animal. I couldn't think about the boot or who it belonged to because right now Kyle and I were in danger of freezing to death.

I finally had the door shut and locked against the storm and any unseen predators, and then I had to work my way through this scene with calm. How was I going to stay calm when Kyle was unconscious? Was this a head injury only manifesting itself now? An aneurysm? His heart? I fell to my knees next to him, checked his pulse, which was steady, and watched as he opened his eyes, blinking slowly.

"Hiding," he mumbled. "You weren't there. You weren't there!" The accusation stung—what had happened to him when I wasn't there? Was this in Boston? What was going wrong? He had to know I'd be there for him whatever happened.

"I'm here now, Kyle." I cradled his head and helped him to stand after a short time when he screwed his eyes shut. "Come on, babe, let's get you up now." He gripped me, and I had to strain every muscle, so we didn't end up tumbling to the ground, since I was the only person keeping us upright. He was limper than a noodle, confused and saying random words that made no sense, but finally I managed to get him to the sofa, and he slumped back into the corner, still with his eyes shut.

"I need to remember," he whispered, his voice changing so he seemed more in control. He pressed fingers to his temples and opened his eyes—his expression bleak. "It's gone."

I sat next to him, took one of his hands and held it tight.

"What happened?" I asked, and he closed his eyes again before making a frustrated sound of impatience. "Kyle?"

"I had this thing…" he waved his other hand at his eyes, "it was right there, and it hurt."

"What thing?" He wasn't making any sense. "I need to check you over—you might have a concussion."

"No!" he snapped at me. "I'm okay!"

"Okay." I attempted to extricate my hand in case he needed space, but he held on so tight I thought he'd cut off my circulation.

"Shit, no, I'm sorry, ignore me. What happened?"

"I don't know, you're the one who fainted."

"I fainted?" He looked so shocked, and a niggle of concern began to worm its way into my thoughts.

"What do you remember?"

"About what?" Jeez, shock had turned very quickly to confusion, and I could see the panic in his eyes.

"What were we doing?"

"We had... we made love, and it was perfect," he murmured and gave me a shy smile.

I wanted to kiss that soft smile so bad, the fact he'd felt it was as perfect as I did had to mean something for both of us. I couldn't, though, because we had more serious things to work on. "And after that?"

He blinked at me, and the panic began to grow in him, agitation in his posture, and his eyes widened. "After?" His breathing quickened, and his free hand pressed against his chest where his panic lay. I needed him to stay calm and focused, and the kinds of things I usually did, like touching him and holding him close, weren't going to get me any answers anytime soon.

Then inspiration hit me—he was icy calm in net. He was the immoveable object, the man who focused so hard he could calculate a hundred different plays and deal with each one of them. When we'd first started skating together, we were both going to be first line centers. Even if we had to take turns to be on the wing, it was us against the world, with dreams of the Stanley Cup and a contract with our nearest NHL team in Winnipeg just there for us to reach. It soon became clear that Kyle was better in net, and finding that out happened entirely by accident. We had this visiting goalie, Aubrey Campbell, a local hero from three towns over, who came to give pointers on playing in net, and he literally changed Kyle's life.

No one on our little team *wanted* to be a goalie. Every single one of us had dreams of the glory of the flashing light, leading our future NHL team out to play in game seven of the Stanley Cup final as captains and goal scorers that ended up in the Hall of Fame. But no, Aubrey arrived when we were maybe eight, and he'd decided our entire under-nine team needed to learn how to focus. All of us giggled and snorted our way through what I now know were beginner visualization classes, and that was how it went for the longest time. I mean, what eight-year-old didn't find lying on their backs and imagining a color spreading into our chest the funniest shit ever?

All except Kyle, that is. He had this uncanny ability to lie still, to calm his breathing, and he explained to me he could visualize colors in a way that made no sense to me. He told me that night as we huddled up in his bed that he saw scarlets streaking and melding with violet. He spoke about the brilliant oranges and yellows that filled his thoughts, and he amazed me. Somehow, he'd changed that week, and for a long time, the dreams that plagued him had slipped away. It hadn't lasted long, but suddenly our team had a goalie who idolized Aubrey, and who helped our team toward a sequence of successes that propelled us upward in our small universe.

He'd been born to be in net, born with that goalie focus that makes the impossible seem possible.

That was where he needed to be because his breathing was harsher, and this was a panic attack he didn't need right now.

"Who is the worst player to defend against when you're in net?" I asked, and he stared at me, his hand screwing at his T-shirt and the panic right there in his eyes.

"Huh?"

"What player do you fear?"

"No one," he muttered, the words slurring.

"There must be someone who gets the puck at the far end. They're spinning around your defense like a top, they pass through legs, they get past everyone, they're heading your way with the best slapshot in history."

"No one," he repeated, but his words seemed clearer.

"They're on your blue line, but their winger is blocking your view, you know that shot is coming, and there's only one person who you know might get it past you—"

"Tennant Rowe," he blurted. "He's fire and passion, and I have to…"

"What? What do you have to do?"

"I settle into my skates, I already know he's the best I

face, him or Tate Collins, they have this way of getting into my head, so I settle." The scrunch of his T-shirt eased as his fist's hold loosened.

"Tell me what you do next."

"It doesn't matter if I'm blocked, I can hear the skates, the crowd just dies away, it's a connection with the ice..." He let go of his T-shirt and rested his hand in his lap, his breathing slowing just a little. "Sometimes I close my eyes, just for a second, and I visualize what is coming for me. Tate can be predictable, fond of top right." His hand moved a fraction as if he was imagining the move. "Tennant's trajectory is like this rush of power and speed, and when I close my eyes, I'm running a hundred scenarios and then I'm seeing nothing, I'm just focused."

Finally, his breathing settled.

"Close your eyes," I said softly and leaned against him. "Tell me about how you feel when you're standing there waiting."

He closed his eyes as I told him, and then he smiled. "Facing Rowe? When I stop one of his shots, it's like I'm king of the whole freaking world—Collins too—but then I have to face the wraparound. The focus is still there until maybe Xander or Joaquim get that puck back up the ice. It's also the gentlest of feelings, despite the action, and it's like pride in a job well done, a relief."

He snuggled into my side, and I put an arm over his shoulder.

"Close your eyes and tell me about the colors."

He chuckled and pressed a kiss to my chin. "That again?"

"I used to love lying with you and listening to you tell me about the things you saw in your thoughts, all the flashes of brilliance, like the Northern Lights in your head."

One last kiss and he totally relaxed. I waited for a while as he flexed his fingers in mine, then he slackened his hold. How he did this I don't know, but somehow, he could find a space inside himself where he was at total peace, and it was that which I had desperately hoped would keep him safe in Boston. Had I been wrong? Was it stupid to have stayed here when he might have needed me by his side?

I was supposed to love him. Had I failed him? He'd mumbled about hiding, and that I hadn't been there—I should have been in Boston with him.

"It's beautiful in my head," he whispered. "All I can see is gold, the same as the flecks in your beautiful eyes." He smiled, and I felt it against my skin. "It's all I see when I think about you, gold, and then I feel warmth. It was the same when we made love just now. But I'm hungry…" He stopped and wriggled a little. "We talked about stew? Wait, I asked you about stew. We were going to eat."

"Yes," I said, hoping to encourage.

"And then… there was a noise, snarling, a thump. What was that? We should check it out."

"We did."

"We did?" He sounded so unsure.

"Some animals were out there, fighting on the porch, maybe looking for shelter, nothing we couldn't handle."

"You saw that?"

"I opened the door, but the storm is vicious, so I shut it quickly."

"What animals would be out in this storm? Wolves?"

"Maybe, I don't begrudge them shelter here, as long as they keep a distance when I open the door."

"You didn't see anything then?"

I hesitated a moment. "Some blood, the remains of an old chewed up boot they'd been fighting over."

Suddenly, he was silent. It was as if I could hear his thoughts racing. "I was hiding," he said softly and buried his face in my neck for a moment. "I was hiding, and you weren't there."

"Where, K? Where was it that I wasn't there? In Boston?"

"No, when I was hiding."

"Where were you hiding?"

"Here, I was little, looking up at things, and the size of them. I know I was really small."

"Was this when we played hide and seek? Did I forget about you and leave you somewhere? I bet it was the time you broke my Millennium Falcon, and I left you hiding in that closet for a whole ten minutes." I was attempting to lighten the tone, but he stiffened in my hold.

"No, I was hiding, and I was small, and then… nothing." He sighed a full body sigh, and I just held him close. "Maybe it was *before*."

Before meaning the time leading up to when he was five, a blank space where he had no memories. Not that everyone recalls being one or two, but there will always be certain childhood memories that stick around. Like, I remember the day the two of us stole the apple pie from his mom's kitchen table to eat, and how sick we'd been after eating it all. We'd been just four. I recall the first time we went on ice on tiny skates—I think we were three—and there are photos to back up the event. One that his mom has in her hallway right next to the one of him in Boston colors when he signed contracts. He looks at those earlier photos, and they mean nothing to him.

He doesn't even recall the time we had our first sleepover at my house and ended up crawling out of my window and sleeping on the roof, staring at the stars. God, my mom was so pissed that we could have slid off, and let's just say we never did it again. We'd both been four. It was the week before Kyle's fifth birthday, and I know that because I was grounded and couldn't go fishing for his birthday.

The small memories that make up the tapestry of our lives are all there to recall at the weirdest of moments. Only Kyle's just don't exist. Experts called it all kinds of fancy names, all ending with the word amnesia, and believe me, over the years I've done my research. There was no trauma that I'd seen, and we'd been joined at the hip from the moment we woke to the moment we slept— closer than brothers. So, all the experts called it infantile amnesia, which was just a fancy way of explaining that adults can't always recollect early childhood memories because their brains were still developing and sometimes unable to consolidate memories.

I still don't believe that a mind as brilliantly creative as Kyle's, and as focused, could have any issues like that. But what do I know?

"Did you bring the boot inside?" he asked after the longest time where we just hugged and breathed together.

"I was more worried about keeping the animals and the snow out, and focusing on the fact that my boyfriend had collapsed at my feet." *Shit, what did I say that for? Why did I use the B word? The L word has been said, but the B word is way more than just simple love.* For me, love is real, and boyfriend is forever and could become husband. That would mean changing our lives, me going to Boston, me finding a way to do that for him until he was done with his career, and then maybe we came home and…

Little steps, Christian, little steps.

"Is that what we are?" He moved away from me so we could look at each other.

"What?" I pretended not to understand because, you know, *self-protection.*

"Boyfriends? Again? As we used to be before I fucked it all up and left you here?"

"I decided to stay, Kyle, it's not all on you."

He frowned and then cradled my face, and I couldn't resist covering his hands with mine. In the cabin, with the wind howling around us, I heard nothing but his breathing.

"You never stopped being my boyfriend, my partner, my forever."

"Jeez, Kyle, way to make a grown man want to cry," I grouched.

Then he kissed me, and I didn't want to cry at all. I lost myself in the embrace and forgot all about the animals, and the boot, and the storm.

TWELVE

Kyle
———

THERE WAS NO DENYING THAT SOMETHING WAS GOING ON
inside my head.

I'd never had a flashback so intense. And I'd never
fainted before. Ever. That freaked me out. What freaked
me out even more was the knowledge that Christian was
now outside retrieving a boot. I waited by the back door
with a deer rifle in my hand as he waded out into the
whirling snow, his head down, his thick winter coat
covered in flakes, the black bear hat old Mr. Smith had
given him pulled down over his ears. My head was clear
now, my focus locked on the mounds of snow. The safety
was on the gun, and I had experience with firearms. Most
people around here did. When you lived where polar bears
chilled in your front yard, you knew how to use a gun.
We'd hunted as kids with our fathers. I'd not used a rifle in
a few years, but it was kind of like riding a bike. You never
forgot. Rifle resting in my arms, snow and ice particles

scouring my face, I watched the tree line for any signs of wildlife coming for us with malicious intent.

"Get the boot and come on back," I murmured as Christian waded out into the blizzard, hand shielding his eyes, to try to read the tracks in the snow. He turned back quickly, cheeks red from the cold and wind, then waded back to the front porch. I hustled him inside, closed the door, and unloaded the firearm before propping it beside the door. Best to have it close at hand just in case whatever had visited made a return trip. "You look frozen."

"I'm fine," he boasted. Well of course he was. We'd not admit if we were cold. We were Manitobans. We never got cold or scared or admitted defeat to the elements. Which was probably part of the reason I felt I could drive through one of the worst storms in forty years. "Could use a cup of coffee though."

I nodded and made my way into the kitchen while he stripped off his outerwear and snow boots at the back door. Thankfully, the power had stayed on. So far. I made two new mugs of coffee and carried them out into the living room to find Christian bent over the boot, which he'd placed on the coffee table after laying out a plastic tablecloth.

"Here," I said as I walked up beside him. He glanced at me, his eyelashes wet with melting snow and his hair flattened down by his fur hat.

"Thanks." He took the mug, sipped gingerly, and turned back to study the boot.

"Did you see any tracks that you could identify?" I

asked as we stood there looking at an old work boot. Snow had removed most of the blood on the outside, but there were marks, and inside the boot where it had been protected, there was the darkest stain of all. I shuddered.

"Wind and snow have covered most of them, but I'm guessing it was coyotes or wolves." I bobbed my head in agreement. "Sounded like a short squabble between some canines."

I sipped, and pondered on the boot and my reaction to it. Where the hell had I witnessed images of scarlet blood? Why was everything so damn dark inside my head? What could I have seen that had made me bury it all so deeply? A shudder ran through me.

"Hey, are you okay?" Christian placed a hand on my arm. I gave him a wobbly smile.

"Sure, yeah, fine, just thinking about that time we found that dead polar bear cub when we were kids. Remember how the conservation officer said they suspected the wolves had learned how to hunt bear cubs?"

"Yeah, I remember that. Takes a really brave or really hungry wolf to take on a mother polar bear."

My mind darted back to that day and the small carcass we'd stumbled across while searching the shoreline of the bay for fossil rocks after the summer thaw. There wasn't much left of the cub, just some white fur and a few scraps of desiccated meat. We both had cried a little that day thinking about the poor mama bear mourning her lost baby. Which was probably the reason our mothers were so damn protective. It always made me blue to think of that mother bear wandering alone.

"Remember how Clyde Friesen acted like such a jerk about it all? He wanted the claws and teeth and threw a fit about not being able to take them," I enquired.

"Loony Clyde is out there being weird, always has been."

"I stopped by the bluff next to his property on the way in." Christian gave me the oddest look. "I know, it was probably stupid, but something called to me. He used to have all those signs posted around his property, but we'd sneak onto it to go fishing and you'd draw dicks on all his warning signs."

Christian laughed. "Oh yeah, I did do that. Well, Clyde is a dick. I see him now and again in town. Looks more and more like some unhinged mountain man every year. Took us a call to the RCMP two years ago to get access to his land to rescue a lost hiker. I mean, shit, I understand a man wants privacy, but to be that paranoid as to let a young woman possibly die?"

"Didn't he use to hang around with Poor Man Pudge?"

"Yeah, they were pretty tight. Sat outside the post office talking about conspiracy theories. Poor Man died last year while outside tending to his hogs. When his son found his body a few days later, it wasn't a pretty sight. Wolves or bears got to the corpse."

I continued to stare at the boot as I pondered on Poor Man, Clyde, and some of the other wingnuts that called Eagle Ridge home over the years.

"I think I'd like to put a call through to my folks? If that's okay?"

"Oh yeah, of course. I'll fire up the ham radio. The cell service dropped out so probably the tower toppled, or the snow is scattering the radio waves. Hopefully the antenna for the ham radio is still holding on up on the roof."

"We'd have heard that come down though, yeah?"

"Yeah, we would have. I was just being an asshole." He gave me a crooked smile.

"Pretty typical behavior for you." I stole a swift kiss. He gathered me close, nothing sexual, just a loving embrace. Fuck, I had missed his arms around me. We stood there wrapped around each other for a long time. The snap of a log in the fire finally broke us apart. He cupped my cheek, searching my gaze for something that I prayed he would find. Must have because the corners of his lips curled up and he rubbed his thumb along my cheekbone.

"I'm so happy you're back."

"Me too," I concurred, his palm warming my stubbly cheek.

"Let's see if we can rouse the old folks."

He led me to the small table by a window where his radio system sat. Most of the search and rescue personnel had one of these. Cell service was awesome. Except when it didn't work, which way out in the wilds was often. Ham radio was old-fashioned, but pretty damn reliable for the most part. My father was a big ham radio buff and had introduced us boys to it years ago. Pops talked to people all over the world.

The transceiver and tuner were stacked atop each other, the microphone off to the side. He sat down and began searching for the proper frequency as I stared at the poster tacked to the wall with all the US and Canadian amateur radio bands and their power limits. My father's call signal was strong, and within seconds, he had replied to Christian's call.

"NV 890, this is BY990," Christian said into the mic. "I have someone here who'd like to talk with you. Are you able to receive, over?"

A burst of static then my father's deep voice boomed out of the rectangular external speaker hooked up to the main radio components.

"BY990, this is NV 890, and we'd love to have a talk with the someone." I got a little choked up. Christian smiled up at me, stood, and offered me the chair. I sat down, gaze clinging to his for a moment, then reached up to pull the desk mic closer and placed my finger on the Lock-To-Talk button on the base.

"Hey, Pops," I said as Christian padded off to the bedroom and closed the door to give me privacy. "It's really good to hear your voice. How's Mom?"

"Mom is just fine," my mother chimed in, making me grin. "How are you?"

"I'm okay." I opted out of telling her that my shoulder hurt. It should be in the sling, but we'd gotten kind of sidetracked with sex and boots and falling back in love with each other. Not that I'd ever been out of love with Christian…

"You don't sound okay. You sound sad. Are you having dreams again?" Mom asked.

I shook my head then recalled she couldn't see me. "Not really," I lied. I glanced back at the boot lying on the table, the strings short and chewed, the toe coated with dried blood. I wasn't sure what exactly had hit me so strongly and had a thought to pump my mother about my childhood, but to what end? We'd been over my amnesia a thousand times with several doctors and mental health professionals. Nothing ever seemed to come of counseling other than discussing my sexuality or team dynamics. "I'm just tired. Sleeping in a new bed and all that."

"Are you sure that's all it is?" Mom prodded because that was what mothers did. Worry.

"Yeah, just fatigue. And the shoulder aches a little bit." Again, I kept things light. They didn't need more to fret over. "Tomorrow is Christmas Eve Day. If this storm ever ends, I'll get to your place. I have your presents with me."

"Don't worry about pushing out before it's safe," my father interjected. "Roads are closed from here to Marmot Gorge. Power's flickering in town. We have plenty of food and firewood though, so we're not worried if it does go dark. You two boys just stay put until it's safe to drive. God knows we don't need another car wrapped around a tree."

"You're so lucky, Kyle. If something had happened to

you…" Mom croaked. I choked up. "Well, we're not going to go there. I'm not ready to hand you over to Negafook."

I chuckled lightly at the name of the Inuit snow God. Then I bit back the snigger. Probably I shouldn't push my luck with the Gods given how things were going. Car wreck, fainting spells, bloody boots, roaming packs of predators.

"I'm not ready to meet Negafook either," I replied as lightly as I could. Mom seemed better after that, less emotional, and we chatted for a few minutes before Christian came back into the room on tiptoes. "I should go now. Give Christian time to raise the Mounties." My gaze resting now on the boot.

"The Mounties? What do you boys need the RCMP for?" Dad immediately asked. I grimaced.

"Just to check in with them about any search and rescue calls he might have missed overnight," I replied. The lie was dismally bad, but I'd never been great at thinking on my feet. "His radio blew a fuse, and we just got it fixed."

Christian's face was pulled into a wince, but thankfully, my parents seemed to buy my terrible lies. I told them I loved them and I'd touch base tomorrow. After our goodbyes, I sat there staring down at the microphone stand. It felt good to talk with them, but there was still the specter of the boot not ten feet away.

"Hey, let's get some food into us then you should rest." Christian's voice pulled me out of the otherworldly place I'd been in. Memories and recollections were thick as fog on the bay. I glanced out the window, into the nothingness of snow and wind, and wondered if the shadow men were on the prowl. Or if it were perhaps a snow God, that was creeping around. He was surely blowing up a big wind outside. Was he in cahoots with the unseen, making it impossible for mortals to leave their homes, thereby giving the shadow men more opportunity to strike? "Hey, are you okay?"

I startled out of the fog. "Fine, good, just thinking about Negafook."

"He's a blowhard," Christian tossed out. "Let's have lunch. Then I want that arm back in the sling and for you to take some pain killers and rest."

Knowing he'd not quit until I'd been fed and clucked over, I gave in without any fight. I really *was* tired, my shoulder ached, and my head was still a little muzzy. We enjoyed a light lunch of canned tomato soup and grilled cheese sandwiches. Christian had taken out a caribou roast to make for dinner. After the midday meal, I washed down some Advil, stretched out on the sofa, and pulled up some goofy romcom with David Spade and Lauren Lapkus. My head was not ready for anything heavier than a romantic comedy. Christian tossed the quilt over my shoulders, kissed my head, and then went to the ham radio to try to raise the Mounties. We did have a potential clue to a death lying on the coffee table. He'd wrapped it up in an old tarp, but lying there on the couch, blanket cocooned around me, my sight kept drifting from the so-so movie to the boot. Even though I couldn't see it now, I'd seen it before.

My eyes got heavier and heavier, the sound of the wind seemingly slowing mingled with Christian calling out to any law enforcement to respond over and over. Perhaps the barracks in the town of Hudson Bay had lost its antenna. I drifted off to David Spade's voice, my body finally giving up the fight to stay awake. The dream didn't start off immediately. I eased into it, like slipping into a warm bath, only the water I was in was not in a tub.

Nor were there any bubbles or candles. It was a pond, covered with bits of leaves, the water chilly and lapping at my knees. There was the smell of fall on the air, a crisp bright aroma that made me yearn for some of my mother's winter squash casserole. The sun was setting, but I could see the yellow perch swimming by. I had no worm on my hook, and so I'd waded out to see if I could catch a fish with my hands. I'd seen Hank Migishoo do an exhibition on it once during an outdoorsman seminar I'd attended with Pops.

With my cold kneecaps and my little boy hands, I moved closer to a fat perch spending his day lazing in a patch of sunlight. Smiling to myself as I neared the unsuspecting fish, I lunged at the perch, my hands cutting into the crystal-clear pond like knives. Water splashed up into my face, the metallic taste of pond scum on my tongue as I grabbed the slippery fish around the middle then hoisted it up out of the water with a shout. Shaking the water from my face, I blinked to clear my eyes. My fingers were tight around a bloated, gray human ankle. A hand grabbed my calf under the water before I could shriek properly. Mouth filling with cold pond water, I was jerked under the surface, the rotted gray face, eyes long gone from the perch picking them out, was right in front of me. I screamed, but nothing came out but air bubbles.

"… Kyle! Kyle, come on, wake up. Wake up!"

I swam up out of the dream with a shout that strained my vocal cords. Terrified and winded, I fell to the floor on my left arm, the pain helping to snap me out of the nightmare. Christian was right there, dropping down to the floor to help me up, then holding me tight as the tremors waned.

"You okay?" He pushed some damp hair from my face. I nodded. He didn't look as if he believed me. I got to my feet with his help, my stomach feeling acidic from the soup and scare. He got me settled, then sat down beside me to check the stitches in my shoulder. The man was a first-class worrywart. "They look good, nothing bleeding." He patted the tape back into place, his gaze meeting mine. "I have to make a quick trip up the road to perform a wellness check on Wilber Smith. I'll be back in less than an hour. You just sit here and—"

"Are you out of your mind? As if I'm letting you go wandering around in a blizzard alone."

He sighed and set his shoulders. Which was fine. I was used to facing down men who were determined to score on me. I sure as hell could hold my own with the man I loved.

THIRTEEN

Christian

As the crow flies, the Smith cabin is maybe a little over half a mile. By road, it would take an hour, down the mountain and back up the mountain on one of the hairiest switchbacks in this area. Walking, it's not so bad on a fine sunny day. In fact, spending time with Wilber had become less a part of my responsibility as a good neighbor, and more about a true friendship. I could sit and listen to his stories for hours, and yes, on a sunny evening, a ten-minute stroll on the incline, crossing the brook with the stone, admiring the views, and then heading back down the other side of my property, was a fine way to end the day. Being outside in nature, with the fresh air and knowing there would be good hot coffee and a few exaggerated stories of days gone by, was a boon for my soul.

Being busy had stopped me from thinking about the things I couldn't have.

Like Kyle.

Now, he was behind me, and I wanted to think about him and what we had, but it was far from a sunny day, and thinking was nigh on impossible. It had taken ten minutes to get out of the damn cabin, and the sweat that I'd worked up was now an uncomfortable chill against any exposed skin. Last winter, one of my projects had been to build a connecting shelter from house to garage, but that didn't help when the drift was ten feet, at least, and steadily accumulating against the door.

"Next summer's job, a bigger wind break," I muttered as my shovel finally hit the base of the door and I could scrape away enough snow to be able to open it.

Kyle followed me in, lines of exhaustion around his eyes. He'd tried his hardest to help, but he was on the injured list for a reason. I tugged him close, which wasn't that close at all because we had on so many layers. We were two walking talking stuffed bears, but on the bright side, we were keeping warm.

"You should stay here," I said again. I'd lost count of how many times I'd said that now, and every time, he'd given me that stubborn Kyle stare and wait me out.

"Nope."

"You know the Rebels will kill me for putting you through this."

"All of them?"

"Yep. Management, your PT, your coaches, the entire team."

"I won't let them hurt you," Kyle smirked. "Not that

I'd want to get between Xander and you if he found out you gave his injured goalie a shovel."

"You took your own shovel." I rolled my eyes, and he shuffled into my space, and we hugged as best we could, given the layers.

When we parted, I went straight to the snowmobile, but Kyle wandered around the work benches. It was only at that last minute that I remembered what was in the huge tool cupboard that he was opening. However, I couldn't exactly call him back, and he might as well know how pathetic I'd been for so long. He went still, and I couldn't see him because the damn door was in the way.

"Kyle?" I asked cautiously. Pasted to the back of the door, in the most unused cupboard, there was a history of us. From kid photos to hockey, and then further down, Kyle in his first Boston Rebels jersey, to his first Rebels shutout -- grinning like a loon with his old captain Brady Rowe lifting him off his feet -- to the charity event last year with the team, him all beautiful in his suit. There were even ticket stubs from his first few games when I sat way up near the roof and watched him as he did what he was supposed to do.

I tried to cut him out of my life, but I couldn't, and now all my stupid insecurities flooded back as if they'd been waiting for the moment when he turned around and said he was wrong to want to love me. That somehow my little scene of his life was a step too far.

"Do you remember the donuts? The ones Chloe made and brought to the hockey pond?" he asked from behind the door. I wished he'd come away from there so I could see his expression. "They were so bad we used them as pucks, but only after we licked off all the icing."

I didn't know what to say, but there was something in his voice that sounded as if he was struggling with too much emotion. Stepping toward him, I wanted to tell him anything he needed to hear so that we were together. I'd apologize for collecting photos, for lying that I never thought about him, for not going down to Boston. Hell, I'd take the blame for everything, my fault or not, just for him to look at me and tell me he wasn't freaked out.

"I remember them."

"If you open my locker, the one we shove our street stuff in, there's a whole load of photos there, of Mom and Dad, Eagle Ridge, of you. Lots of you. Me and you together, you on your own, and there's this cutting from a Winnipeg paper from three years back, when you were part of that river rescue and got that commendation."

My heart slowed, just a little, from its fast pace—Kyle had a similar wall of photos connecting us? Maybe I wasn't such an idiot.

"Okay."

"But the best photo of us is when we were twelve." He shut the cabinet door and, finally, he was looking at me. His eyes were shiny with emotion. "We were posing with those damn donuts, the day that Chloe hung around and we had to go through the motions of eating them."

"You have that photo."

He closed his eyes briefly, then nodded. "I'll make you

a copy. We're both in Winnipeg colors. You're a head taller than me, and you're smiling. It captures everything from that day because I'm staring down at the donut, and you can see from my expression that I'm really not looking forward to eating that rock-hard fried monstrosity."

"They *were* bad, I'll give you that." *Still not following this.*

"You pretended you loved them so much that you ate mine as well."

"I did?" I genuinely didn't recall that, but it must have been an important memory for him to remember that.

"That's what you did, you made things easy for me; you took all the bad parts of my life, the nightmares, the shitty donuts, the fights with other kids, and you protected me from it all. I want you to know that I loved you for that, and I still love you for that." He pressed a hand to his chest, on top of the many layers of clothing against his skin. "Aside from Mom and Dad, you're the only person who truly knows what's in here." He tapped over his heart. "All the big things like my stupid freaking nightmares and fears, and the simple things like not wanting to eat donuts, to how high we could climb before we jumped into Eagle Lake. You know *me*." The last part he said so fiercely that I immediately went to him and kissed him as best I could, yanking off my gloves and pushing aside his balaclava so I could cradle his cool skin.

"Forever," I muttered into the kiss.

"Forever," he repeated and kissed me back.

"Whatever it takes," I added, and God, I meant it.

We smiled like idiots and then went about checking over the Cat before pushing it between us out the door and into the snow. In the time we'd been in the garage, it had stopped snowing, heavily at least, and instead, there were soft flakes swirling in the air—the kind you can taste on your tongue, tiny crystal shards that connected me to this land.

"Ready?" I asked and shoved the door shut before climbing on the snowmobile. As I dug, I'd piled the snow in a temporary ramp and patted it down, but beyond the cabin, the thick snow was compacted enough so that if we could get a good start we'd be up and out. Then we just needed to navigate the stream, hope it was completely frozen and the gulley was filled with a shit ton of compacted snow, then we'd get down to Wilber.

Kyle clambered on behind me, holding as tight as he could with one arm. I worried about his shoulder briefly, but then imagined the heated debate we'd have if I insisted he stay here. He had a rifle, and I was armed. We had emergency supplies and five hours of daylight. Easy.

The feel of soaring across the snow, weaving past groups of trees, the snow no less deep even under cover, was freeing. I heard Kyle whoop behind me, which made me let out a whoop of my own. If anyone saw us, they'd think that two kids were out there shouting in the snow— they weren't wrong—I don't think either of us would ever grow up, and anyway, this was one way to scare off any animal that wanted a taste of us. Although I'm not sure "whooping like idiots" was in the search and rescue manual. There's nothing like skimming and beating the snow, and for the first ten minutes everything went well… that was until we got to the stream and the large trees had rooted and twisted into the only passable part. The stream had existed here forever, carving a drop of eight feet at least, and I'd really hoped the snow had made a natural bridge, but even though the drop was nearly full of snow as far as I could see in either direction, the dip was obvious and the snow was loose, and I knew we wouldn't make it over.

I killed the engine and frowned. Even though the Smith place wasn't far now, it was still going to be hard work. We could probably slide down, but getting back up, well, that was going to be hard.

"We're walking the rest of the way." I clambered off and removed snowshoes from the storage, along with all the supplies we might need. Rifles in hand, we trudged through the snow to the two logs that formed a bridge over the stream. I knew exactly where they were because I knew this area like the back of my hand. I gestured that I was going first. "Step where I step," I ordered, and Kyle didn't argue. Neither of us were going to play games with Mother Nature, nor fall into hidden traps. Cautiously, we made our way over the bridge to the other side, and then with unspoken agreement, we headed down. Each step was hard, and the snow began to swirl again, more insistent, but this wasn't another storm, it was just snow whipped up by the icy wind. At least the trees gave us some shelter, and finally, the Smith cabin came into view, only the roof visible from this angle, smoke curling from the chimney.

It wasn't a wasted journey to check on him though, because he hadn't checked in with the RCMP after his sister couldn't hail him, and he was my reclusive, slightly odd, exaggerating about everything, friend. My tension at connecting in my mind the bloody boot to Wilber dissipated—he was in there, probably with some of his awesome coffee, reading his cowboy novels, and would be surprised to find us on his doorstep.

"He makes the best coffee," I shouted back at Kyle, but when he didn't answer, I turned back to see that he'd stopped six paces back and was staring at something off to the side. "Kyle?" He wasn't pointing his rifle at whatever it was that had caught his attention, so I wasn't worried it was something out to hurt us, but standing stone dead in the middle of gusting wind that whipped up sharp ice and snow wasn't the best idea. "Kyle?"

He didn't move, so I reversed my steps, sliding and stomping my way over to him as he'd moved slightly off the main path I'd made. He glanced at me, and all I could see was his eyes, his lashes frosty, the rest of his face covered by a scarf. I didn't need to see anything else because his eyes were wide with shock, and then he pointed. I turned the same way he was, focusing on where he'd pointed, and at first, I couldn't see anything.

I expected snow, there was snow. I expected drifts in the trees, and yep, there were drifts, piles of snow that would melt in the spring and feed into the streams that collected and ran into Eagle Lake.

"What?" I asked, keeping my tone easy. If this was a specter of his nightmares that had jumped out of the snow, then I was taking my care of him very seriously. Gently, I touched his arm, and he startled, and I looked again. Snow. Drifts. The twisted trees that had in their young lives been hit by lightning. They were beautiful like two people embracing. They'd grown in such a symbiotic fashion it was hard to tell which tree was which. I scanned the ground, and then I saw something blue, material maybe, a thin sliver of color against the white, and I covered my eyes to stop the wind in them and focused. More than a sliver, there was a ball of material in the twisted cage of the two trees.

At first, I couldn't comprehend what I was seeing, and why it had freaked out Kyle so much. I took a step closer. Then another. Sinking deep in the snow, wading past the grabbing bare branches that tried to impede my way. The closer I got, the more I was certain I knew what I was looking at.

The remains of a person, frozen in place, lodged in the trees, and with their back to me. There was very little left, if anything, that might have protruded out from the tree, limbs gone, most of the head…

I knew.

I just knew.

Wilber Smith.

And I stumbled back to Kyle, reversing my walk, my

rifle cocked, alert to everything around me. Whatever animal had eaten him could well still be here, too much meat left there for any predator to resist. What did I need to do? How long had he been there? I needed to cover him with something. I needed to…

Bile filled my throat and I vomited into a bush. In all my years with rescues, I'd only ever witnessed one human death, a young girl drowned, peacefully floating in crystal water, barely bruised.

This was different—this was brutal and ferocious—and I couldn't breathe.

Kyle touched my arm, he yanked me back on the path with his good arm, he raised his rifle and checked around us.

"We need to cover him, retrieve him, help him," I said in a rush, my chest tight with grief and shock, and my head filled with pain. He was an old man whose family would want to bury him. They'd want to make sure he was at peace. What kind of peace had he gotten when he died? Had he stumbled out in the snow, lost his way, been dragged to where he was now? He should have called me —I would have come over and helped. I bet he'd been getting wood or stubbornly scraping snow.

"Christian?"

"Huh?"

"How long has he been there do you think?"

"I can't tell. Days, maybe a day, it won't be more than three or four, I saw him before the storm, had coffee, he told me about his cousin who he said was one of JFK's bodyguards. Tall tales that was all, but he believed them, and he would tell me so many…"

Kyle shoved at me to get my attention, and this time, he was pointing at the cabin.

He leaned in. "Not hours then?"

"No, at least… no… not hours."

"Then who is using the cabin? Why is there smoke rising from the chimney?"

Grief and shock slipped away in an instant, and I immediately went into rescue mode. This could be a hiker lost, finding a cabin, someone who needed our help. I went back on the main path—the living had to trump the dead in this instance—and I headed through the snow to the main cabin, slipping and sliding down the last slope, catching myself at the bottom. I was aware Kyle was following me at a slower pace, but finally, we were both at the cabin door, which opened just as we got there.

"Come in!" Clyde Friesen called over the wind.

What was he doing in Wilber's cabin? And wait— Clyde was smiling at us.

Clyde never smiled at anyone. He was grouchy and territorial, a man who didn't brook anyone on his land.

Next to me Kyle had frozen in place, waiting for my reaction probably. I shifted my hold on the rifle, calling attention to the fact I was armed.

"What are you doing here?" I asked, a hundred reasons flooding my thoughts—maybe he'd been up here visiting? Doing his own kind of welfare check on Wilber? They weren't friends, and Clyde was never a man to show kindness to any soul. Still, standing there in jeans and a sweater, half hidden by the door, he looked less of a demon than I recalled -- old, grizzled, and amenable.

"Got caught up here, visiting with Wilber, you know how it is. He's making stew—come in out of the cold."

Kyle started to say something, but I knocked his elbow and stopped him.

"Can we talk to him?" I tensed when Clyde moved the door enough so we could see inside the cabin.

"Stove's warm." He smiled again, but it was forced, his lips stretched over crooked teeth, more a grimace than a warm welcome.

Kyle took a step back, attempted to grip my arm, and I swear he whimpered. Clyde's expression changed immediately, and now he wasn't smiling, but grinning insanely.

"I knew it was you," he said with glee and pointed at Kyle, the manic expression making me take my own step back, rifle raised. "You remember it all now, don't you?"

"We have to go... Christian... please..." Kyle moved even further back from the door, yanking at me to get me to move. Distracted, I glanced at him and stumbled a little. A crack broke the swirling wind and pain bloomed in my shoulder, knocking me back and off my feet, my rifle dropping. Kyle looked terrified.

"Drop your weapon, kid," Clyde demanded, and Kyle tossed his gun, then shielded me from Clyde. He was waiting for a bullet. Did he want to die along with me? Why wasn't he running?

"Run." I wanted to push him, but my arm wouldn't move, and blood stained the snow around me.

"I'm not leaving you."

"You have to run—"

"No."

Then Clyde's voice boomed over the sound of rushing in my head as he collected our rifles and tossed them in the house.

"It's all very heroic, but I'm giving you fifteen minutes head start, and you'd better run because I'm hunting you both." He curled his lips in a snarl. "Time's ticking, boys."

We stood there stunned, my shoulder on fire, life blood leaking out of me. "What?" Kyle asked, his voice as weak as I was beginning to feel.

"You heard me, Lourenco. You know what you saw. Can't have that getting out, so sorry."

The door slammed shut on his face, which was blurry as I blinked in pain.

We had fifteen minutes to run.

FOURTEEN

Kyle

IF EVER THERE HAD BEEN A TIME THAT I'D FELT UTTERLY useless, it was standing on that porch with Christian bleeding out. My head was a maelstrom. Images and sounds spiraling around inside my skull. Dark visages— shadow man—prowling past… a bloody boot… what the hell did it all mean?

I might have spun totally out of control if not for the grunt of pain from Christian. He leaned into me, saying something. I shook away the unseen to focus on Christian. This I could do. Right? God what if I couldn't?

You got this. Just focus. Find your center and focus. This is like hockey. Concentrate and block out everything else. He needs you to be the strong one now, Kyle. Don't let him die. Don't let him slip away from you again. FOCUS!

"… to my cabin," Christian was saying, his hand over the entry wound in his shoulder, mittens slick with fresh red blood. Something nipped at my memory. A pond… a cabin… a hand coated with viscera… a hollow under a log. "Kyle, we need to staunch the blood."

"Yeah, of course." I slid an arm around him, and panic was riding my back hard, its grip tight on the nape of my neck. I needed to find my core, the center, the place where I went before a game.

"Loony Clyde has gone deeper into the rabbit hole. Fuck, this hurts." Christian grimaced as I led him up the hill. "Get into my pack." He rested his ass against a fallen tree and shifted his shoulder to get the bag he'd taken from the CAT. "Use the long-range walkie-talkies. We can probably raise Carter Barbier. His place is about four miles from here. I think… I think that's the edge of the range for the handheld."

"Right, keep an eye on the cabin." My heart was pounding so loud I was having trouble hearing Christian speaking. Or perhaps he was growing that weak. I studied him.

"Hurry. I'm fine." He had his hand up under his coat, his face a mask of pain. "Think it went through. Christ, what the hell is—" I pulled out the shattered bits that used to be the walkie talkies. "Fuck! What the hell!"

"The bullet went through? That's good right? Maybe you just fell badly to destroy the walkie talkies?" My thoughts blew apart like dandelion fuzz in a summer wind.

"He said you saw something. What?"

"I don't know what he was talking about!"

I gaped at the things in my hands as if I had no clue

what they ever were. Damn my screwy head! I had to focus. I drew in a breath, let it out, and gathered Christian to my side.

"We're heading to your cabin?" I asked.

"No, he'll go there first," Christian replied, then tore a strip off the blanket and wadded it up under his coat. "We'll take the old fire road to the switchback. It's a rough go, but that will slow him down, too. Once we make the fire road, we can drop down into the valley, follow the creek along to the old fire station, then bank left to find Carter's place."

Carter. Yeah, I knew him. He'd gone to school with us, just a year behind. He was one of two reporters who worked for the Eagle Ridge News, a small paper that went out once a week. How they even had enough news for a weekly run was beyond me.

Christian glanced down at the snow. It was dotted with red. He crammed another ball of blanket up near his shoulder. I did the same on his back, choking back the feel of the warm blood oozing out of the much larger hole in his upper back.

"This is insane," I mumbled, easing my arm around my lover then guiding him in the opposite direction from his cabin. The wind was howling again, no snow, but gusty blasts that shook the trees, a small blessing that the wind was covering our tracks—a bit—but was stealing heat from our bodies. "This is insane. Why is he doing this?"

"I think maybe he killed Wilber."

"And we're witnesses?"

Christian kept up the pace as well as could be expected. I had no idea how much time had passed. My eyes were watering from the wintry wind and the nightmare we were living. "We need to cut over to the west here."

We moved around a huge pine tree and began a slow climb up to the fire road. The small trail, made just for fire management purposes, was also used by hikers, hunters, and dirt bike riders. Ten minutes had to have passed. I kept glancing over my left shoulder, ignoring the pain and pulling taking place inside me. It was Christian who I was worried about. My injury would, at worst, just need refixing, if I pulled something free inside. The man I loved might die.

We trudged onward, snowshoes aiding us in our escape. I kept wanting to check my phone for service, but knew it would be futile. Service this far from town was dicey on a warm, sunny day. With a raging storm blowing out of the area, and towers either down or coated with snow and ice, a cell signal would be "as rare as hen's teeth" as Pops would say. Shit. I wished I'd spent more time with my parents. They'd not done anything wrong. I'd distanced myself from them—from this whole province —because I was scared. What a miserably cowardly thing to do.

"I have to rest…" Christian gasped after we'd pushed slowly up a steep rise. The sign for the fire road lay just ahead, all coated with snow. "He's going to find us too easily." I propped him against a tree, glancing back down the knoll, anxiety at critical levels. There was no blood on the fluffy white snow, but there were tracks. Big, bold ones.

"We'll keep ahead of him. Just catch your breath." I took the blanket from around his shoulders, ripped off another hank, and replaced the soggy wads of cotton under his shirt. My gloves were covered with blood, frozen and wet. I stared at Christian. He was pale, his cheeks pink from the wind and cold, but the flesh under that was sallow. Panic biting into my neck, I glanced around nervously. "We need to get you fixed up better. Is there a—"

The report of a rifle sounded off, just as a chunk of wood and bark exploded not two feet over Christian's head. We both yelped and went to our knees, Christian moaning in pain as he slid to the snowy earth.

"I'll get you, Lourenco. It's been a long wait, but I'm hot on your trail now!" Clyde bellowed from somewhere. Where the hell was he? I shoved Christian down lower into the snow, his breath and mine hot bellows of steam.

"Fuck," I mumbled, resting my head on Christian's soaking wet toque. "Sit tight."

"Kyle, no, don't do something stupid."

"I'm not," I lied, kissed his tight lips, and then moved along the ground on my hands and knees, my head suddenly clear. Perhaps it was the bullet whizzing by or the simple fact that I was all done with Loony Clyde trying to kill us for no damn good reason. Maybe someday I'd be able to figure out why this insane old mountain man was out for my blood. Right now, it was all about survival. I'd be damned if I was letting Christian die out here in the tundra due to some mad conspiracy theorist lunatic. Snow coating my belly, I crawled around rocks and trees, the boreal forest thinning a bit here, as it had been controlled burned a few years ago. Shifting behind a charred stump, I peeked around and caught a flash of orange. Oh, awesome. So fucking Clyde had worn his hunting gear so he didn't get shot while hunting down two innocent men. That rat fuck bastard. Anger now clawed at my insides. It was a caustic mix of ire and terror that spurred me on. The old man in the bright orange coat and cap stood out like a sore pecker. God, I hoped I would see my father one more time. I'd kiss him and beg forgiveness for the years of distance. Mom too. And Christian.

God above, please let the man I love live. I'll gladly give you anything in exchange for his life. He's a good man. This town needs him. I need him. Just let him be okay, and I promise I will dedicate every game to you until the day I retire. Amen.

Keeping low to the ground, I kept moving, inch by inch, Clyde's coat a beacon in the white wilderness. When I was within perhaps three meters, I could hear him huffing and coughing into his hand as he battled to catch his breath. Forty years of smoking will do that to a man. Now I could smell him, the rank stink of cigarette smoke that clung to his outer garments. Bet he never shot a caribou or moose in his life. The stench of tobacco would scare away any animal in its right mind. I ran my hand along a dead tree, found a stout branch, and snapped it off.

Clyde peeked around the tree. I drew back and took a swing, aiming for his head. If I stoved his skull, I didn't care. I'd worry over facing a murder charge later. Right now, it was kill or be killed. His rheumy eyes went wide, and he threw up the .300 Remington to block the blow. The gun went off, shattering the snow-coated boughs of a long dead fir tree. Was the man that stupid that he was walking through the woods with his finger on the trigger?

"Fucker!" Clyde snarled, whipping around with a speed I'd not expected in a man his age and poor shape. The butt of the rifle caught me under the chin. I saw stars, but stayed on my feet, lunging forward to try to wrest the rifle from him. Blood warmed my cheek. His eyes were wide and manic, his breath thick with cigarettes and bad teeth. "Fucker, miserable little spying fucker!"

I brought up a knee, catching him in the balls. That sent him down and then backward. Rolling ass over tin cups, he tumbled down the rise to land in a small divot. Watching in pleasure, I was sure he had to be winded, if nothing else. But no, the madman shoved to his feet, brought up the rifle, and popped off a round. His forehead was bleeding profusely. I saw it before I dropped down to avoid the shot. It went wide. I looked down cautiously, using the blow downs and mounds of snow as cover. He cursed me in French as he tried to climb back up and failed, his leg buckling under him.

"Fucker! You'll pay for this!" He roared then fed

another bullet into the gun. The second shot hit closer, but was still off the mark. I'd not taken him out, but I had slowed him down, perhaps given us some time. Knowing he would be working at making it back up to me, I took off, snowshoes eating up the distance. Christian was where I had left him, his eyes wide with panic as I slid into the small nook where I'd tucked him safely away from prying eyes. There were empty bandage wrappers on the snow as well as sodden clumps of bloody blanket. At least he'd used the time to good advantage.

"You stupid fuck!" he spat, then grabbed me by the neck and crashed his cold lips to mine. "Stupid ass. I heard shots. Fuck, I thought he had gotten you. Stupid ass!" He patted my cold cheeks, his beautiful eyes watering, then kissed me one last time. "You have a cut," he said as he tipped back my head.

"I'm fine. I slowed him down a bit." I stood and then hoisted him to his boots, both of us groaning from our injured shoulders. "He's wounded. Head and leg, but still armed. We have to keep moving."

"Don't you *ever* do that again. Do you hear me?" he growled; his fingers fisted in the side of my coat as we began pushing through the snow toward Carter Barbier's place. "I'm all over you leaving me. Got it?"

"Yes, sir, I got it." I had no plans on ever leaving him again. If push came to shove and he refused to leave Manitoba, I'd quit the Rebels and get a job taking people out to whale watch. Maybe I'd need a better canoe than we'd had as kids, but that was something to worry over later. "I'm never leaving you again."

"Good. Dumbass."

With the specter of Clyde hounding us, although at a greater distance and with a limp, we kept moving. Our speed began to wane though, as Christian grew weaker and weaker. Four miles is a nothing distance for me. I run that plus on a treadmill every other day. Now, four miles felt like a thousand. Christian was growing heavier and heavier with each step, his strength leaving him, putting more of his weight on me. He could barely lift his feet with the snowshoes on, so we stopped—again—to take them off and I ignored the pain as I shoved them under my free arm.

"You should—"

"If you say leave you, I will kick your ass, bullet holes in you or not," I panted, jerking him up higher, leading him along one plodding step at a time. I threw him a look. His lips were pressed tight, his gaze a little muddy. Fear clamped down on me like a Doberman.

"You should tell me a story," he said as I corrected my hold, his arm around my neck heavy as a sandbag. My thighs were burning, my back cramped, my shoulder and jaw weeping blood. Yet there was no stopping. We'd not even made it to the abandoned fire tower yet. There were still two or so miles to traverse. Hopefully, the swirling winds would help to obfuscate our tracks in the snow and keep all the hungry polar bears out on the bay.

"Okay, yeah, a story." I wasn't sure we should be making more noise, but he was slipping quickly, his grasp on consciousness weakening. If the sound of my voice kept him with me, then I'd talk myself hoarse. "I remember the first time I met Stan Lyamin. We'd been down to Pennsylvania to play a game in their barn. We'd gotten into town just before an ice storm. The game wasn't even delayed or anything. Guess people in Pennsylvania are used to bad weather, just like us Manitobans."

"Yeah, it's… they do cold in there," Christian groggily replied.

I tamped down my panic and continued the story he had asked for. "The game was a tight one. The Railers are good, you know. Tennant Rowe is a demon. He's got this move that few goalies can handle. It's like this tiny little jerk to the right, a twitch of his hand, that leads you to that side, then he makes his move. He's got a killer deke. Anyway, he got me twice with that move. I was fit to be tied as your mom would say." That got a gruff sound of amusement from him. Snow fell from a branch high above us; the wind picked it up as it fell, filling the air with a million gleaming diamonds. It would have been pretty if my boyfriend wasn't dying. "We ended up losing in OT. When the game was over and we were all leaving the arena, Stan came meandering up to me. This was my first year in the league, and you know how I idolized Lyamin." Christian muttered something incomprehensible. "Exactly, totally my hero. So, there we were in this busy hallway, and he smiled down at me, offered me his hand, and shook mine and said, 'Always keep the worm in your pocket when you are picking up the shoes from the lake.'"

"What does that even mean?" Christian asked, the sound of his raspy voice joyous.

"I don't have any idea." I chuckled softly, and Christian did the same. We walked through the cloud of snow dancing on the wind, and I stopped. There in front of us was a jagged rock face, several meters high, that would take us hours to circumvent with Christian so weak. My heart dropped when I saw it. A small cave, the opening nearly obscured by snow. Christian began to slip. I snugged him to me. "Luxury accommodations ahead. We can look at your wound. You with me?"

"Always…" he whispered before going lax in my arms.

FIFTEEN

Kyle

It's amazing how fast a man can move when fear is propelling him.

After gently easing Christian against a tree, I dove at the snow covering the cave opening. Even calling it a cave was a stretch. It turned out to be nothing more than a small nook, barely big enough for two men. Using my hands to clear the way, I stuck my head in slowly, sniffing the air in case a bear had denned up here. Thankfully, there was no animal hibernating inside the tiny lair. Gathering Christian up from the ground where he'd slipped, I did my best to wedge him into the grotto without hurting him. His hisses of pain showed that I'd failed him. Which wouldn't be the first time, but if I didn't do something smart, it might be the last. I'd spent my adult life thinking only about me, my fears, and look where it had gotten me. Alone and being hunted by a raving madman filled with rancor. A rancor I had no fucking clue about or could even recall stirring up.

How could I have harmed Clyde? I'd never even spent time around him. My mother and father had warned me away from him, saying he had "issues," but never detailing what his "issues" were.

"Sorry, sorry. I know it hurts." I tucked Christian back as far as I could, helping him to stretch out his long legs for comfort. Crouching down, my knees on the cold earth, my head resting on the rock ceiling.

"If I ask you for a promise, will you make it to me?" he enquired sloppily while I pulled up his coat and shirt. Both were slick with blood.

"Of course," I replied, my attention on the task at hand. We had a few bandages left. His wounds were oozing blood, so I dug into the baggie, finding four gauze squares, a roll of white tape, and one of those little hand-warmers. I tore the hand-warmer open, then placed it in his hands after removing his wet gloves.

"Leave me here."

My gaze flew from the bullet wound in his shoulder to his face.

"I'm not leaving you." My reply was short and firm.

"Then we'll both die." I shook my head, focused now on tending to his wounds. "Kyle, listen to me." I shook my head even more strongly. "Kyle." His voice was weak. I peeked up, tape in my hand, to find him smiling at me. I wanted to cry. "Kyle, I'm going to die if I keep moving."

"You'll die if I leave you here. You'll freeze. No, I'm not leaving you."

"Kyle, I won't freeze. I have this hand-warmer." As if

that would be enough to keep him warm. "If you leave me here, you can reach Carter's in half the time. He has an Argo. He can come get me. You can lead him here. You have to go. I can't take another step."

"But…"

"Go, please. I'll be fine. I'll be warm enough. I can rest."

"What if a polar bear finds you?" Yes, I was terrified and grasping at straws.

"They're all out on the bay hunting seals." Fuck, he was calm. Tears welled. I dashed them away and said nothing as I taped a clean bandage to his front and back. He sat there silently, his breathing steady if a bit shallow. "Kyle, you promised."

"Fuck you, that promise was made under duress." But deep down I knew he was right. Clyde had to be closing the distance. I'd not stopped him, only slowed him down. I wiggled the hand-warmer up under Christian's coat, placing it on his chest to hopefully help keep his core warm.

"Kyle…"

"Yes, okay, I know. I'll go alone!" I snapped, then instantly felt bad. "Sorry, I'm just…"

"I know. Go, go now. I'm fine. Keep moving northwest. When you spot the fire tower—"

"I skirt Eagle Bluff, then drop down into the gorge, keeping a wide berth of Clyde's land that buffets Harrier Lake."

"Yeah, I don't think… you have to worry about Loony Clyde coming out with a shotgun to chase you off."

No, I guessed not. He was coming on our trail with a deer rifle and a grudge. I did the best I could for Christian, pulling in handfuls of clean snow that he could put in his mouth for water when he got thirsty, then going out into the bitter cold wind to snap off pine boughs with which I covered him the best I could, leaving only his head out. I knelt beside him, cradling his face in my wet gloves, scared to leave him, yet scared to stay.

"Go, I'm good." He gave me a wobbly smile. I kissed his lips.

"Do *not* die on me."

"I won't. Cross my heart. Now go."

It took all I had to back out of the grotto. Knowing I had to get moving, I took the time to drag a bough around the area, trying to cover our tracks before placing the bough carefully over the opening to the rocky nook where the man I loved was hidden. I then climbed upward, using the strong legs hockey had given me to move upward with relative ease and ignoring the tear of pain in my shoulder. It was a blessing the snow had ended, but the wind was still howling, peeling away body heat despite the layers of clothing I wore. Plodding onward, I moved in the direction of the old fire tower, my mind now locked solely on reaching Carter's little home on the other side of the tower. Each step took me further from Christian, but closer to being able to save him.

The woods were white, everything covered with fluffy

snow piled in mounds four feet deep at the base of the trees. My body was mostly depleted of energy now. I was moving on sheer determination and terror, but not because I was scared of Clyde. I was horrified of Clyde killing me and poor Christian dying in a fucking rock overhang. I shook off the thoughts of cataclysmic scenes of impending doom. I needed to be in the proper headspace. A yelp of pure glee nearly escaped me when I rounded some birch trees that had grown close together to see the base of the fire tower. A jolt of energy appeared out of nowhere, spurring me along with a speed that had been waning just a few minutes ago.

I moved around the tower, keeping a hand on the thick wooden beams that served as the base. In the summer there would be teens from Eagle Ridge up here at night, having sex and smoking pot around a fire. Now it was nothing but snow and ice. Snowshoe treads gripping the snow, I made my way around the tower, leaving the images of warm summer nights and laughter behind. It wasn't far now. Perhaps another mile as the crow flies, less if I banked to the left to skim Clyde's property line.

Using the tower to guide me, I moved in the direction of Harrier Lake, a small freshwater lake that ran deep, but wasn't all that big. Maybe three hectares total. Keeping my head down, I hurried along, and paused to catch my breath and eat a handful of snow. My breath fogged in front of me, then was whisked away by the wind. Looking ahead, I saw Harrier Lake for the first time in many years. Off to the side, barely visible, sat Clyde's rundown home. It was an A-frame cabin that he'd built himself. Snow melting on my tongue, a sudden onslaught of memories rode down on me with an intensity that knocked the air out of me. Grasping the rough bark of a red pine, I was whisked back in time…

The lake was calm, dragonflies skimming over the placid water, the hum of honeybees loud in my ears. I was mad. Loony Clyde never mowed his grass. Weeds and wildflowers grew up to the windows he had covered with tar paper. To keep the government from spying on him. Why he thought the prime minister wanted to see what he did, I didn't know. All I knew was that I was alone because Christian had gone to some stupid dance recital for his cousin when he had sworn we'd sneak to the lake to catch perch for my birthday.

"Stupid dancing girls," I muttered, the smell of the lake reaching my nose. Maybe I wasn't so mad at Christian as I was at his cousin Laura. She always pinched my cheeks and called me cute. She was eight to our five. Why did she think she was so old and wise? Girls were dumb. So were moms who made boys go to dance recitals or forbade their sons to go fishing alone. I was five now and knew the woods good. Better than good. Better than Pops or Hank Migishoo. I knew how to find the fire tower and the deer trail to the lake, and I didn't need a grown-up or Christian along. I knew how to stay away from Loony Clyde's cabin. I'd be six soon and starting school. I knew things about the world.

Easing down to the shore, I slid off my sneakers, tossed

them into the weeds, and sat down to dig in the soft mud. Once I found a worm, I stuck it on the hook, then cast out into the cold, dark water. I'd lost my bobber on the way here, but that was okay. I'd sit here like Pops, fingers on the string of my fishing pole, and the moment I felt a tug, I'd set the hook. I knew all about fishing and outdoor things and hockey.

Hidden among the reeds, I dipped my bare toes into the cold water, the summer sun that warmed my head making me drowsy. Eyes heavy, I felt myself dozing. A loud noise jarred me from my nap. I gasped, dropped my pole, and craned my head left and right. Another blast of a gun sounded off nearby, the report echoing off Eagle Bluff so high above. I threw my arms over my head and went to my belly. Maybe Loony Clyde was shooting at a deer out of season. He did all kinds of bad things because of his "issues," according to the grown-ups. Shaking, I lay flat down on my belly. I could hear Clyde now, muttering as he did when he came upon me in town. He hated kids and dogs and the government. What a dog had ever done to him I didn't know—all dogs were good dogs. Heart slamming into my ribs, I shimmied along on my belly to the blown down tree that lay half in and half out of the lake. Whimpering, I wedged my spine into the root ball, dirt rolling down my back and into my hair.

"... fucking spies," Clyde growled as he passed by. I drew my knees to my chest then covered my mouth. "I know they're watching me. This fucker ain't watching nothing no more."

He passed by close, so close that I could see the red splotches on his work boots. He smelled bad. Like a stinky man who never washed. I smashed my fingers together to block off the stink then watched, eyes wide, as Clyde walked out into the lake pulling a body behind him. The body of a skinny man in red hiking shorts. I knew it was a man, as the body had no boobs and his shirt was rucked up to what remained of his chin. The man's head was a mash of blood, pulp, and bloody bone fragments. I squeezed my eyes shut as tight as I could make them. There was splashing, cursing in French, and then... nothing. Just the hum of honeybees and the windswept lap of the water along the shore. Throw up rose high in my throat. I swallowed it down as Clyde slopped his way out of the lake. Biting down on my palm as he took a step closer to the roots, I nearly bit through my flesh when he bent down to pick up my child-sized fishing pole. I pressed back into the dirt and roots. He never looked under the clods of soil. Perhaps Agloolik had been watching over me. I had been fishing, and he did help hunters and fishermen. Mom would say it was so.

"Little fucker," he growled, then bellowed. "I know you're here, little fucker! If I ever get the chance, I'll carve your spying eyes out. You hear me!"

He stormed off, taking my Zebco rod and reel. I didn't move until it was dark. I wet my pants during the afternoon, but I stayed there under the root ball, too scared to move from my spot. I cried silently, my legs cramping as the sun shifted in the sky, the moon chasing the sun as it did daily. The longer I sat there, the less scared I was. When it was dusk, I crawled out, my thoughts confused. Why was I here at the lake? Where was my pole? I looked at Clyde's house, wood smoke from his cookstove curling up into the night sky. Why was I here? Did he know why I was here? I didn't think he would tell me even if he did. He was mean to kids. I plodded off, barefooted. Had I worn shoes? I made my way along the lake, cutting the soles of my feet on rocks and thorny plants, unsure of which way to go to get home. When I hit the road I walked down it, scared because the world was big, and I was small and lost. I crawled back into the house and Mom found me curled up in bed. She'd been so angry because she'd been scared—I'd never been gone for that long before, and worst of all, I'd been alone.

She asked me where I'd been.

The treehouse, Mom.

I'd lied, and the memories had become part of a lie, for much of my childhood.

Other random odd flashes of memories appeared. So many questions throughout the years, and never once did we put me out playing in a treehouse together with losing my memory. Zero answers. For years. Zero answers. Bile rose in my throat. I swallowed it down and blinked to clear the tears blurring my vision.

The report of a rifle jolted me from the horrors of my past. I jerked, dropping down instinctually as deer do on occasion. That movement probably saved my life, as the shot meant for my head caught me in the arm instead. I'd have to thank my years of mental training to be a goalie for that later. If I didn't die here in the snow. Holding my bloody arm, I lowered still, moving from the open and fading back into the trees. Using a fir for cover, I glanced back and caught a flash of movement. Clyde, still in his orange gear, was trying to haul his ass up the rise. I waited, head filled with so many warring ideas that it was hard to keep my goals straight, until he moved by the tree I was hidden behind. This time, when the bastard moved close, I didn't hide as I had as a child. I whipped around the tree like an enraged polar bear -- all teeth and fists and years of pent-up rage and nightmares -- and leaped on the madman. He tried to bring the gun around to shoot, but I ripped it out of his hands, then clocked him with it. The butt of the gun hit him in the forehead, busting open the skin. I kicked him in the stomach, as hard as I could, and he windmilled back a step, eyes wide, mouth open, and plummeted over the bluff. His scream echoed for just a brief moment, then the wind lifted it up and blew it away.

Blood dripping from my fingers, I made my way to the edge of the bluff, looking down the seventy or so yards. There at the bottom lay Clyde, his body twisted, in a pool of crimson.

"The unseen is now seen and is only a sick, murderous man with no soul," I mumbled before I turned from the sight and vomited into the snow, using the backs of my bloody fingers to wipe the puke from my lips. Unable to take the time to mentally process what had just taken place, I pushed onward, leaving a bright red trail in my wake as I trudged onward. Time was a meaningless thing for me as I fumbled along, my snowshoes carrying me to the small clearing where Carter Barbier lived.

Woodsmoke met me first, the smell of sweet white birch leading me to the front door of his doublewide. I tripped going up his front steps, my snowshoe catching on the stairs, and fell into the door with a grunt. Carter's voice could be heard from behind the door. He opened it to peek around at whomever was on his stoop.

"Good God, Kyle?" my old schoolmate asked, his bright gray eyes round as dinner plates. "Did you run into a bear?"

No, something far more evil.

"We need help!"

SIXTEEN

Christian

THE ONLY THING I KNEW WAS ICE AND SNOW. IT BLOCKED
me in here, it swirled around me, and a clump of it melted
inside my clothes right against my wound.

Snow will be cold enough to coagulate the blood. I
don't know where that thought came from, and I don't
know if it worked because one touch of the freezing snow
and I lost consciousness. Or at least I think I did. I wasn't
sure of anything right now. I heard noises outside, but they
were in my dreams, whispers that Clyde was standing right
outside, his rifle pointed at me, Kyle bleeding out in the
snow, dead.

What was the point in living right now? I just wanted
Clyde to get over with everything. Maybe someone would
come up here and check in on me, but what would they
find? An empty cabin, with the monopoly board still
strewn over the kitchen table where we'd set it up for
when we got back.

"I don't plan on playing games," Kyle had whispered against my lips, but I saw him hide Park Place right under what had become his side of the board. I was going to get that back when we went home.

If we went home.

Am I home? Is Clyde here? Why is it so cold?

Kyle. I love you. I'm sorry.

I tried to close my eyes, but someone was stopping me, telling me to open my eyes. I didn't want to. I was numb to pain, and my heart was slowing to the point that I could just close my eyes and drift away. At least Kyle had hope —I'd sent him away. Told him it was okay to leave.

"I've got a pulse, he's alive."

My last good deed was to save the man I loved. In my fevered imagination, he made it to Carter's place, and he got help, and even if it was too late for me, I knew Kyle would be safe. That had to be the best thing I'd ever done in my life. Something shoved at me, and I whimpered, thrusting my hand out and smashing something hard. Snow blocked my view, surrounded me, and I didn't know which way was up and which was down.

"Open your eyes, Christian."

I couldn't, my body was heavy, and I was caught with a heavy weight on my chest. I shoved again, but it was nothing at all against whomever was attempting to root me out of where I was huddled.

Kyle needs me to stay here. He needs to find my body where he left me. For closure.

"Maybe it's better he's out of it."

Who was there? Was it Kyle? *You should have run, Kyle. Why are you here?*

"On three. One. Two. Three!"

Agony knifed through me and icy snow filled my mouth when I screamed—I wanted the bliss of whiteness where everything was painless. Sound faded in and out, and someone kept asking me to open my eyes, to stay with him—it was a voice that was dear to me. Kyle was here. Kyle was alive?

"Is that okay? Got him? Let's move." Hands poked at me, something jostled me, and the world swung sickeningly. I closed my eyes tight shut, screwed them closed to keep the world away, but I swore Kyle was talking to me.

"I've got you, Christian. I've got you. I'm here."

Then another voice. "Shit, this is impossible. What the hell?"

God, was it Clyde? Where is he? Run, Kyle!

I hate being ill. It doesn't happen to me often—I'm fit, young, and a cold doesn't stop me from running the store, or going out and helping people. I had the flu once, proper flu, the kind that wiped me out for a week or more, but I'd only been little, and then it was my mom holding my hand and keeping me safe. I felt like that now, as if I'd been picked up like a ragdoll and thrown off a mountain, tumbling end over end to a crevasse below. I couldn't breathe, I couldn't stop the fear in my thoughts, and I needed to know what was happening.

I needed to know that Kyle was okay.

"Kyle?" my voice was scratchy, the single syllable lost on the exhale of a breath. "Kyle!"

"I'm here, it's okay. I'm here."

"Clyde?"

"Dead. It's okay. He's dead."

He took my hand, and I tried to grip it, but the bright lights and the whiteness around me took me under again.

The next time I opened my eyes the pain wasn't as intense, instead everything floated on fluffy white clouds. I moved my fingers and wriggled my toes, assessing the levels of hurt and finding that nothing hurt at all. Not a good sign. I was either back in the snow frozen, dead, or I was drugged up something good.

"Hey."

I turned my head slowly to face Kyle, who was sitting at my side, leaning forward in his chair, one hand on the cover, the other arm in a sling. He was smiling, or at least half smiling, the smile didn't reach his eyes. No, there lay worry and fear, and I didn't want him to fear anything. I tried to reach for him, but I couldn't move, so I tried to talk.

"Hey," I managed after a few attempts and several ice chips that he gently placed on my tongue. For the longest time, he stared down at me, then he smoothed my hair back from my face and pressed a kiss to my forehead.

"I thought I was going to lose you," he murmured in a broken voice, and the next kiss was just to the corner of my mouth.

"You shouldn't have gone back for me." I tried to

move my hand to touch him, but realized it was weighed down, and I panicked. It seemed as if everything hit me at once. "Why did you come back?"

"It was safe. Clyde's dead."

"For real?"

"For real."

I nodded at the sling. "Is that from him hurting you?"

"He tried, winged me, but luckily the same arm as my shoulder injury, so only the one sling."

"He shot you?" *If he wasn't already dead…*

"He tried… it just made me so fucking angry… he slipped and tumbled over the edge at Eagle Bluff. I didn't shove him, not really, I was defending myself, but I didn't help him. He was trying to kill me." He sounded so shocked, and I knew his expression must have mirrored my own.

"Why?"

He closed his eyes and shook his head. "Shit, Christian, there's bodies, so many bodies."

"Huh?" Off the cliff? Nothing was making sense after the flood of relief at hearing Clyde was dead, and when I'd ascertained that Kyle wasn't seriously hurt. My injury throbbed now, but I wondered if that was me allowing it to hurt now that I knew Clyde wasn't a threat and I could come out of fight mode?

As if I could fight anything right now.

"No, on his property, there's an old well, a mine shaft, they don't know how many, they're trying to tie names to… I must have seen something. I began to recall, had flashes of a body, of him dragging someone through water, but it's still hazy. The doc says I repressed the memories to keep myself safe, and I think flashes of memory came back to me when I had to detour down the old road to get to town. You remember I said that I stopped by his place on my way up here?"

"Yeah."

"Well, something in here must have begun to work." He tapped his forehead with the hand on his bad arm and winced. "As long as I didn't remember, I guess I was okay, but he saw the way I was staring at a certain point, and somehow, he knew I suspected, or God knows, because I don't. He just wanted to add me to his list of the dead."

"Why are there bodies? What did he do?"

Kyle bit his lips, and I swear he went so pale, I wondered if I should call a nurse.

"He hunted them for sport, like wild animals."

"I don't understand, why didn't he try to kill you before?"

"I don't think he knew it was me, or even if anyone could have seen. I'd blocked it out. My mom remembers the day I said I'd been playing in the treehouse, barefoot with cuts, and how I'd been so quiet, but she'd put it down to her being furious I'd been gone all day playing outside. She didn't know, I didn't know, he didn't know. All that ignorance kept me safe all these years."

"And then you stopped your car at his place on the way in, and that was enough to make him think you suspected something?"

"It was something he said to me. It didn't seem important at the time, but I talked about fishing there with you, it's not even fully on his property. He talked right over me, told me to move along, and I did because fuck… Loony Clyde is fucked up."

"Case in point…" I glanced down at my chest, swathed in bandages on one side as if I was some weird half mummy. "I don't feel so good…" I coughed and yelped as the good stuff had started to wear off, and pain was my new best friend.

"I'll get the doctor," he said and went to stand, but I clenched my fingers around his and yanked him to stop. It wasn't my best move, as every single one of my muscles screamed in protest to the movement.

"No leaving," I demanded, but the words were weak, and I couldn't stop him even if I tried.

"I won't be going far."

"Stay." I could be stubborn when I needed to be. Particularly when I was afraid that if he stopped holding me, he would disappear, and I would wake from this warm dream state.

"Okay, I'll wait until your mom and dad come back from the cafeteria. They shouldn't be long, but I sent them down when your mom looked as if she was going to fall asleep on the floor from lack of sleep."

"Wait, how long has she been here?" *How long have I been out of it?*

"She hasn't really moved far since we got you here."

"How long?" I repeated because words were failing me, and now even breathing hurt.

"Four days. I went back for you with Carter, and we got you down to his place then called in help from Search and Rescue, it was... panic, pain..." He pressed another kiss to my forehead, and the small part of me that didn't hurt pleaded for a proper kiss to give me proof of life. If we kissed, then he wasn't dead, and I wasn't dead; this wasn't some fucked up medically induced fantasy. "They had to warm you up, but that was a good thing because hypothermia slowed the bleeding. They couldn't operate at first, but they did yesterday, and..." He stopped, and then he buried his face in my neck. "Fuck, Christian, fuck."

"I need..." He moved, and the pain was too intense to ignore. "Doc..." I wanted to be brave and ignore the pain. God, I wanted a kiss as well. I closed my eyes, and there was a flurry of motion, the touch of hands, and then a coolness into my hand from the cannula and the fluffy clouds were back, and it was beautiful.

I felt better each time I woke. The next time it was to find Mom and Dad next to me. Mom fretting, Dad stoic and telling me all the details of how he was covering the store, even though it was still officially shut, as the storm that had dumped the snow was followed by another slower pass and had cut off town for a couple more days. I listened to Dad ramble on, held Mom's hand, and was never happier than when they finally removed the cannula and told me that, all being well, I'd be out of the hospital the following day, if I had help at home. Of course, Mom immediately said I was going home with them, and I even began to explain that I had Kyle, but then Kyle himself interjected from the door.

"It's okay Mrs. Gauthier, I'm good to look after him."

She sent him an affectionate, but exasperated glance. "And who is going to look after you?" she demanded. "Both of you will come to our house for a delayed Christmas celebration, okay?"

I wanted to be with Kyle. Selfishly I wanted to be in his bed, cuddling next to him and recalling every single inch of him. It wouldn't even have to be sex. I just wanted to hold him and know he was okay. I didn't want to be in my childhood bedroom and for him to be in the guest room. I wanted to be open and honest about *us*. Kyle beat me to it.

"We're together again," he announced and rounded the other side of the bed to lean there as close as he could.

"And?" Mom prompted.

Kyle was flustered. "Well, we'd want to… Christian?"

"Mom, Dad, we'll be holding hands, kissing, hugging, and we'll want our own room… together."

Mom and Dad exchanged glances, and then Dad smirked.

"We know that." Mom huffed an exaggerated sigh. "Which is why your dad tidied up your room and moved the king bed from the guest room. That's your room now. Yours and Kyle's. Also, can I just say, boys, it's about time."

With kisses and hugs and Dad explaining how he was

going back to check on the store, they finally left. At last, it was just me and Kyle. I patted the mattress.

"Come here," I demanded.

"Ready for hockey?" Kyle asked as he nudged me over in the bed and situated himself so he could cuddle into my side, the TV remote control on my chest.

"Which teams are playing?"

"No idea." He switched on the TV and flicked around to find the right channel, and even I could see from this weird angle it was a Boston game. He was lying if he didn't know it was Boston, and that small slip forced my thoughts to much more pressing matters. It didn't matter if my parents were fully behind me and Kyle being together, or if Kyle's parents were the same. What mattered is that my life is here in Manitoba, and Kyle's is in Boston. I didn't say anything about the fears in my heart.

"You had to know it was Boston/Railers, right? That's a big game."

He mumbled something low in his throat that I didn't catch, but it sounded suspiciously like he said he didn't care.

"Kyle?"

He sighed noisily. "I spoke to my agent, Marissa, I mean."

"I know who Marissa is," I teased. She was the one who helped him decide that it would be wonderful to leave Canada. *Bitter, much?*

"She spoke to the team. They were supportive and understanding and extended my time here, but…"

"But what?"

He lifted the remote and muted the enthusiastic pundit discussion about the Rowe cousins match-up. Then he sat quietly for the longest time, and I didn't push him at all. Even glancing at his expression made my chest tighten. He was going to tell me he was going back home, and at this moment I would get up out of this damn bed and follow him down there. I don't know what I'd do, maybe join a local rescue center, or… fuck knows. But I'd find *something* if it meant staying with him, even if it was going to be hell to drag each of my long-buried roots out of the frozen Manitoba soil.

"The doc here spoke to the team doc, and they've agreed to extend my leave, rehab here, heal, but the team owner, Nick Sinclair, has already called up Reuben Gentry from our farm team. All it takes is one half season of good games for Reuben, and I could lose my place on the Rebels for good. It's a lot to take in."

"I know." I laced our fingers together. "It's not something you need to think about tonight, let's watch Boston kick the Railers' asses and you can pack my stuff to take me home in the morning. Yeah?" I didn't want to see him frown. I wanted to see his beautiful smile, but there was no sign of it as he lapsed into silence when the teams lined up. They were playing Reuben in net tonight, and I could see the intense focus behind his mask on close-ups. I didn't know much about him, only that he was older than Kyle and had played for Boston a way back before going down to the Essex Schooners, the Rebels farm team.

He had to be close to retiring and surely, he wouldn't be enough to take Kyle's place?

A small voice inside my head told me that it would be a good thing if Reuben took Kyle's spot. A treacherous voice. I should want what was best for Kyle, and if that was going back to Boston, then that is what I wanted.

Right?

SEVENTEEN

Kyle

_____

THERE ARE MANY REASONS FOR PEOPLE TO CELEBRATE Christmas Day arriving, particularly celebrating it ten days late and well into January. Most don't revolve around the fact that a person was still miraculously alive, as was the man he loved, and that going back to his parent's house meant a break from law enforcement.

I'd never seen so many red-coated police officers in my life. Growing up, we'd occasionally see a Mountie, usually when someone did something wrong. Like that time Peter Allooloo tried to stuff Wally Edmunds into an ice-fishing hole headfirst when we were in high school. Seemed Peter and Wally were both trying to claim Melissa Irnit, who owned the sole diner in town. Melissa was a highly sought-after prize due to her cooking skills and long widowhood. The Mounties arrived, pulled Wally out of the small hole in the ice, and arrested both men. Melissa ended up marrying Marion Gibbons, the librarian over in Marmot Gorge. For some reason, my mother always laughed at the end of that story. What tickled her so about a lesbian librarian I had no clue, but she always giggled.

I had lost count of how many questions I had answered and how many times I'd told the story about my arrival back home. My parents had sat on either side of me when I'd been speaking to the Mounties, and a fancy lawyer from Boston attended the questionings via Zoom. The fact that Nick Sinclair had loaned me one of his expensive attorneys made me nervous. As did the fact that, until the criminal investigations were over and my body and mind were healed, I was now on the long-term injured reserve list. Which was totally understandable. I didn't blame the team at all. I was the one who'd called Nick to tell him what had happened. He'd reacted as I'd thought he would —with a rush of bluster and a few heated Greek phrases. After the initial burst, he jumped into the situation as if he knew all about criminal investigations into dead bodies.

My head was not in a good place, and I was looking at a possible charge for something. Granted it was self-defense, and my lawyer from Boston—Anastasios Galanis —was confident I'd not be charged. I was still a mess. I felt as if I'd killed someone. Every time I closed my eyes, I saw Clyde falling over that bluff, his eyes wide with surprise, his arms spinning. In my dreams, the unseen now had a face, and it was smashed all over the rocky ground of Eagle Bluff. Between that image and the resurgence of all my lost memories, sleep wasn't a friend of mine, even with Mom's warm milk and cinnamon. Seemed the only thing that helped was having Christian close to me in bed, and even with him spooned in front of me, my rest was fractured.

Still, even with all the turmoil, it was now time for our super late-Christmas, and both of our families were gathered in the Gauthier living room, pretending it was a normal holiday. If our folks squeezed their eyes real tight, they might be able to overlook the slings, bandages, and bullet holes both their sons were sporting. We'd had a massive breakfast, and were now sipping eggnog and opening presents. Christian was tight to my side on the sofa, the tree was lit, and the smell of a roasting turkey filled the small home that I'd spent so much time in as a child. Where Mrs. Gauthier and my mother thought we'd put another massive meal I couldn't begin to say. I'd be twenty pounds heavier when I returned to Boston. *If* I returned. My future was up in the air, just like Santa's flying reindeer.

"Oh, I talked to Rocky Qappik last night," my dad said as he handed me a gift. A hockey stick. It was wrapped in gold paper, but I knew what it was. It's hard to disguise a stick. While I could buy any stick I wanted, Pops always got me a new one to add to my collection. "He's got insurance on his wife's vehicle that should cover most of the damage. And plus, he says it was an act of God, so if we owe anything, it will be negligible."

"So, God put that moose in the road?" I asked as I began to gently peel off the paper on the goalie paddle.

"Maybe so," Mom chimed in as the steam from her cup of coffee tickled her button nose. "Perhaps Amarok the wolf God chased that moose into your path so that you'd end up back with Christian."

I glanced at the man beside me. He gave me a soft little smile that turned my insides to jelly. We'd somehow made it through a horrendous ordeal alive. Battered and permanently scarred, but alive. That could certainly be considered a miracle

"Next time one of the Gods wants to interfere, maybe they can leave out car crashes and mass murderers," I tossed out. Mom began to tear up. "No more tears. That was supposed to be a joke."

"You never could tell a joke," Christian teased. "Remember that talent show in middle school? Your act was nothing but bad joke after bad joke."

"They were good jokes," my father interrupted. "It was just Kyle's delivery."

"They were dad jokes, Dad!" I countered, and we all laughed.

That seemed to be enough to break the mood that had lingered over us. At least for a little while. Mom and Pops seemed happy with their late gifts. Probably, I could have given them caribou droppings, and they'd have gushed over them. They were just happy to have me home. A whole me. One that, despite the injuries, now had his past back, dark as it may be. You can't go forward until you know your past. Now that I was in possession of those memories, I could begin to sort through them and heal. Christian and I both had appointments at the clinic in Marmot Gorge to speak to the lone counselor they had. Rural healthcare had some pretty large limitations, especially when it came to mental health. It was important that Christian went as well. He, too, had been traumatized. The man had nearly died. Recalling his blue lips as we pulled him from the grotto made me tremble.

"Hey, no going there," Christian whispered, then draped his good arm around my shoulders. He pressed a kiss to my brow. "Today, we leave all that behind. Just for one day."

"Right, yeah, I'm sorry." I let my head drop to his shoulder. Mom was watching us, her eyes dewy. Mrs. Gauthier cleared her throat, then asked if we could watch something fun and silly. Christian's father dug around in the entertainment center and pulled out a dusty DVD of *Christmas Vacation* with Chevy Chase. As soon as I spied the cover, I began snickering and didn't stop laughing until the end credits rolled.

The folks got up to tend to the holiday feast, forbidding either of us to lift a hand. I was content to simply sit here with Christian as a soft snowy wind rustled around the house.

"I'm still full from breakfast," he confided as we snuggled.

"I know it. I won't be able to skate from one end of the

rink to the other if I ever go back." I patted my belly and sighed dramatically.

"*If?*"

I blinked, then looked from my stomach to my lover. "When. *When* I go back." I gave him a wan sort of smirky smile. "No sad thoughts today, right?"

His expression shifted. "Would going back make you sad?"

I stared at his lips. "Leaving you would make me sad, yeah. But we'll just have to make it work, yeah?"

"Yeah, for sure we'll make it work." He dropped a kiss to my hair, and we switched topics, talking about hockey, which was kind of better, but not so much.

Reuben had taken over my spot like the pro he was. His performance had been flawless, and now, with my name on the LTIR, his position as starting goalie for the Rebels was pretty well secure. Even with my professional life up in the air, I didn't feel any great panic. Once we were cleared by the Moms to live alone again—mothers cared little about what doctors said—we'd be moving into Christian's cabin for the duration of my stay. Or I guess he'd be moving back, and I'd be moving in. In a way, thinking about living with him felt funny and ticklish and new. Yet, in another way, it seemed inevitable. As if my destiny had always been with him in that small cabin in the woods. I'd just not known it. Or maybe I'd been too scared to see it.

Whatever the reasoning, I was looking forward to it. I missed being intimate with him. And not just sex. Neither of us were anywhere near ready for making love. I just missed the quiet times where we were in the same room, but not talking. There had never been awkward silences between us back in the day. I wanted to rekindle that now. I yearned to spend long nights curled up with him watching a movie or taking walks through the woods. Hell, maybe we could fall into the snow and watch the Northern Lights. Maybe he'd kiss me, and we'd find our way back to each other. Maybe we already had. No maybes. Not now. We had found our way back to each other, and I vowed nothing would ever come between us again.

I pecked his cheek. It was rough with whiskers. Neither of us had shaved, and the Moms had given us a pass just this once. Next year at Christmas, we'd better have cheeks like a baby's behind, Mrs. Gauthier had informed us after patting our scratchy faces. Christian held me to his side, and I napped, the sounds of our families chatting in my ears and the firm, warm strength of my man at my side. Christian had to wake me up to eat.

Somehow, we found a few pockets of room in our bellies for a massive feast. The carbohydrate overload was crushing. Spread out on the sofa, bodies aligned so our various wounds were being coddled, Christian and I snuggled close, sipping more eggnog—we loved the nog here in Eagle Bluff—and enjoyed an evening spent dozing on and off while trying to watch *Die Hard*. Yes, it is a Christmas movie. Come at me. I will die on that hill.

Around eleven, we were chased us off to bed. My parents went home, and the house grew still and silent as we disrobed and pulled on some joggers. The bed was big and inviting. I hoped that all my napping wouldn't interfere with my sleep, or what sleep I'd sneak in before the nightmares started. My shoulder ached badly, the new stitches pulling tightly, just as the ones in my biceps were. As Christian stripped, I sat on the edge of his bed, surrounded by a room in which, besides the bigger bed, not much had changed from when he was young. The same books sat on the shelf above a wooden desk, the same posters of sports stars were hanging on the walls, the same drapes hung on the windows, although they were now a faded blue instead of the dark navy they'd once been. My eye caught the spine of our incredibly thin yearbook.

Our classes were so small the yearbook wasn't exclusively for seniors. It had all the classes from the year we had graduated, from little kids first entering school to young adults leaving it. Our school colors of black and yellow stood out along the spine. I thought back to those years, filled with so much agony and ecstasy. I'd lost so much of my childhood, memories of parties and pets and outings. I had no clue if they'd all come back. How far back did a young boys' memory go? Even if I lost one, that was one too many. Clyde had stolen that from me… and much more. The shifting terrors were all down to him and the grisly sight that I'd seen. If only I'd not gone off that day alone and in a snit.

"Are you okay?" I snapped back at the sound of Christian's voice and forced a smile just for him. He didn't buy it. I could tell by the way his brow furrowed. He sat down, clad in warm fleece top and bottoms, his hip close to mine and oh-so warm. "Where'd you go there?"

I could have told him the truth. Told him that I was cursing myself for ever leaving home that day. Not that scolding myself over it would change a thing. The past was gone. The future lay ahead. All we had was the here and now.

"I was checking out the yearbook on the shelf." That much was true, so I wasn't exactly lying. "Remember what you wrote in mine?"

"Something about your terrible flatulent reaction to my mother's bean dip?"

"No, asshole." He nudged me with his shoulder. We both moaned in pain. "Dumbass."

He sniggered softly, his pretty eyes showing his fatigue. He had a long road of recovery yet. As did I. Hell, everyone in town did. Clyde had killed countless hikers and tourists over the years. Bones still needed to be identified. According to the Mounties, it might take years to get an ID on all the remains. It's possible they might never get them all identified. They seemed to think that my run-in with Clyde was heroic, as I'd not only saved Christian, but I'd saved who knows how many others who might have wandered onto his land and never returned. Why he had shot and disposed of so many people had been explained in a manifesto discovered in his home. Along with enough guns and ordnance to stage a coup in a small Latin American country. Every single person in this backwoods part of the bay had some recovery to do.

When evil moved among a town it always left deep wounds.

"Yes, I remember what I wrote in your yearbook," he whispered as the house began settling for the night. "Dear Kyle," he said from memory, his gaze finding mine. "No matter where life leads us, we'll always be two souls with one heart."

"Yeah, that was it. It was perfect."

"Of course. I'm a master of words."

We both snorted at that. I'd seen the grades on his essays. A writer he was not. But he was an amazing man in so many other ways. He was kind, generous, loving, loyal, and brave. He was perfect, just like that short passage in my yearbook.

"I think you were right. That we do share one heart," I explained when he cocked a brow.

"I'd like to kiss you back into that bed and then love you until the word 'think' leaves that sentence and is replaced with 'know.'"

I smirked a little. "I know you were right. We do share one heart. Will you kiss me back into the bed anyway?"

He did. We both groaned in pain, sniggered a bit, and then curled up around each other the best we could and watched the greens and golds of the night sky through his frosty window. With my head on his chest, I wondered if the lights truly were torches held in the hands of the Spirits seeking the souls of those who had just died to lead them over the abyss. Perhaps so, and all the souls that had been locked into the mortal world by Clyde's villainy had now been freed. I found that to be soothing and whispered it to Christian.

"Maybe *you're* the word master," he softly replied.

I had doubts about that. I wasn't sure who Kyle Lourenco was or what he was doing, but I did know that whatever it *was*, he was doing it with Christian Gauthier beside him.

EIGHTEEN

Christian

THE SPECTER OF A TRIAL FOR WHAT KYLE HAD DONE WAS A dark thing, almost as scary as the demons that had chased Kyle to Boston. The crown withdrew all charges by mid-January. His defense counsel was pissed it had taken so long, but some of that was the fact that the media had been involved. In one news report, it was written that he'd lost his shit and murdered someone, in another, he was a hero who deserved a medal, and there were a ton of news articles that sat in between.

The media attention on the town, with only three sets of remains identified so far, was intense, until the RCMP wrapped up everything with a bow and presented it as done. There would be forensic work to identify everyone else buried on Clyde's property, but the man had been eighty, and he'd lived on that land all his life, so who knew what else was out there. Other than this, though, the case was deemed solved when it came to his death. Kyle had acted in self-defense, and the crown wasn't able to proceed with a trial. All charges were withdrawn as they should have been.

Thankfully, as we reached the end of January, the media attention died down, and Kyle and I could breathe. We'd become inseparable for many reasons, and we were living together. He'd taken to coming into the store with me, mostly sitting in the back with a book, but this morning he was out front helping me string paper valentines in the store window. This was entirely his idea, and I wasn't going to argue when something this simple put a smile on his face.

"It looks good," he summarized from his place safe on the floor. I was the one up a ladder, precariously balanced and attempting to fix the last tie to a nail left over from the Christmas display. He still wore a sling—by now the shoulder should have been fixed and done, but he'd torn an internal stitch in his mad scramble to stay alive, not to mention the bullet wound that had exacerbated the original injury. He didn't need the sling at home, just when he was out… if anything to stop people asking him when he was heading back to Boston.

Because that was one question, he'd become a master at avoiding.

It was inevitable that one day he would—the team wouldn't leave him on injured reserve forever—and if there wasn't a place for him at Boston, then there would be a trade, and he'd end up somewhere else.

Winnipeg maybe? That would be the best-case scenario and even that was pretty shit.

I clambered down from the stall—my injury site aching, my arm rotation still not one-hundred percent from the bullet—and stood next to him to admire our work.

I never decorated for Valentine's, the best I managed was Christmas and Canada Day, and that was mostly just some lights in winter and a poster in July. Lots of things were changing the longer we were here together. Another storm hit last week, and this time, we'd been shut off to the world in the cabin, but we'd been happy. The world was full of freaking sunshine when we were together like that —trapped, with nowhere to go.

Neither of us had to think about what came next because there was nothing we could do but stay where we were. Kyle couldn't leave for Boston, and I didn't have to decide whether to stay.

Kyle knocked elbows. "Earth to Christian."

"Sorry, was thinking about…" I waved at the hearts, and he rolled his eyes at me.

"Only you could overthink paper hearts."

"Hey, red-pink-red-pink or red-red-pink-pink is a real dilemma."

He snorted a laugh. "Add in white and you have yourself a real sticky situation."

Then it was my turn to roll my eyes, and I was just about to remonstrate at length about symmetry when Kyle's phone began to vibrate behind the counter. I wanted to tell him to ignore it, but he'd been waiting for a call, and hanging the hearts was only a temporary reprieve. He crossed to pick up the phone, nodding at me.

"It's Marissa," he said and answered with a forced cheeriness, while I turned my back to him and fussed with the remaining paper hearts. I didn't want to hear his side of the conversation because I sure as hell knew that his agent would have a ton of things to say on the matter of him getting back to work. Physically, he was unable to play. Likely, he'd be out for at least another month when it came down to sheer injury issues, longer when his mental health was considered.

"Okay," he murmured, and there was the distant tinny sound of Marissa chatting on about something else. "Yes, I get that," he responded to another statement. I picked up another piece of string and measured it out for the space on the door. Over breakfast, he'd explained that he was going to do a fancy arrangement for the door with the remaining cutouts, but what need would we have for a fancy display? Okay, so we had more tourism now, trickling groups passed through when it wasn't storming and took photos—the grisly kind, the ones that would appear on social media showing the place where the Fisherman had lived. That wasn't my nickname, that was another media shitstorm—calling Clyde that made him into a cartoon in people's heads, some Batman bad guy who could be defeated.

Not one of these tourists gave a second thought to the irreparable scar that Clyde had left on the town.

"Not an option," Kyle said, his tone firmer as he found

his footing in the conversation. "Okay. Let me… yes… I will."

He ended the call, but I still couldn't face him, wanting to give him some space to think through whatever it was that Marissa had told him. He snaked his arm around me and rested his head on my shoulder, peeking over to look at the hearts.

"The psych eval, plus the doc's report, has me off team for the rest of the season," he murmured. I wanted to dance around the room and pump my fist in the air—that meant I had him here until September when he needed to report for training camp. I decided to ignore his ongoing training and the fact he'd need top notch conditioning to be anywhere near the level he needed to be for an NHL game. Rehab could be done here. Right? Thing is, I couldn't be joyful. I had to be the best version of me, and turn in his hold and tell him I was sorry. With resolve, I turned and hugged him gently.

"I know that's not what you wanted to hear," I whispered close to his ear.

"Meh, it's okay, I'm not in the right headspace for Boston or the team. I couldn't even answer a call from Austin, and that is some hiding away level shit."

My chest tightened. "Is that what you're doing? Hiding?"

Pressing a kiss to my neck, then another, he sighed. "I'm busy getting my head straight and falling more in love with you every day—that's not hiding."

He knew the exact words I needed to hear, and I

couldn't help but kiss him, tangling my hands in his hair and holding him still.

"I love you," I said, feeling lighter, happier. The decision we needed to make was delayed again it seemed, and I was happy in that space.

He pulled back from the kiss. "She needs a decision from me though, or at least an indication that I want to go back."

I was confused. "Why wouldn't you want to go back?"

Staring at me and shrugging, he answered, "She's just covering all the bases I guess." I knew he was lying because I knew his tells, or at least I thought I did. He might have changed a lot since going south, but I still *knew* him. "Anyway, let's get the rest of these hearts up. Yeah?" I detected something in his voice as if he was forcing the positive happy side, and I winced. Was me expressing confusion over him going back akin to me telling him to go?

"I want you here as long as I can," I said quickly, and he side-eyed me with a smirk.

"Of course, you do."

I just wish his teasing smile had reached his eyes.

FEBRUARY MOVED INTO MARCH, SOFT AND SLOW, AND Kyle began rehab for real, working a program with his PT back in Boston, the iPad propped up between them so that the man Kyle labeled The Punisher could talk about form.

He could only do this where there was solid Wi-Fi, so we'd converted the back room of the store into a small gym, and each day, aching and battered, he seemed stronger. He changed what he was eating as well—pizza was out, and chicken was in, and by the time April came around, his stomach was flat, and his six-pack was so defined I couldn't keep my hands from it when we made love.

The Rebels made it to the postseason, but ended up getting taken out by a determined Railers team. We watched all the Rebels games in that series that we could get our hands on, but there was a shift in the way he viewed them. He watched the first of the Rebels/Railers clash with disappointment and sadness, and a heaping serving of regret that he couldn't be there to help *his* team. The next game he watched with less intensity, and by the time they lost the last game, he'd become quiet and disinterested. Deadly quiet as he nibbled on healthy snacks and turned down beer.

The last game against the Railers wasn't televised here, and we couldn't find a feed, so we listened to it on a sports radio station. I couldn't fail to notice that Kyle spent a long time wandering off into the garden or finding excuses not to listen.

By the end of June, with his physical fitness enough to take up his role with the team, and with his mental health healing with every new day, he was scheduled to head down to Boston for talks. He didn't elaborate, but apparently this couldn't be done via video and involved him signing documents, or something I wasn't too sure about because he didn't explain. I wanted to go with him, but he didn't ask, and even though we were together, there was still this issue of who went where and why.

I'd researched work in Boston, traveling, sourced support for the store, considered how I could spend a month in Boston, then a month up here, and in the summers, we could spend time here. I just needed to get all my thoughts in order so that I crossed all the Ts and dotted the Is.

"Let's go for a walk." He was already putting on his walking boots, and I quickly pulled mine on and laced them. We went hiking almost every day, down to town, past the lake, out onto the mountain, everywhere aside from near the Smith cabin.

Only, today was different.

Today, Kyle determinedly turned left, and we hiked up to the low stream and clambered over the logs to the other side. Then he stopped as if he'd hit an invisible wall. The town had paid for a small marker where we'd found Wilber's body. The horror that he'd been murdered by Clyde was just another mark in the column of madness, but the town wanted to remember Wilber for the gentle, if not eccentric, old man he'd been. I'd gone to the small ceremony—Kyle hadn't. I could understand why he'd wanted to avoid the cabin, and the memories, and not one person demanded to know why he wasn't there when he was a big part of the story. In fact, every single person in town showed Kyle compassion and support. He'd become part of the book club, an honorary member of the history club, and was spending time at the school, working with the PE teacher in a voluntary capacity. Slowly, I'd seen the hidden parts of Kyle emerge, and I knew it would kill me when he left.

Which is why I was thinking that maybe I'd just leave with him. He had another five years in professional hockey, perhaps ten, or maybe he'd decide to go into coaching, and it was twenty, but we'd always be able to come home.

"Are you okay?" I asked, standing close to him, hoping that our hands touching would give him some reassurance. In answer, he laced his fingers with mine and began to walk, this time more of a stroll down the hill to the cabin. He'd been doing a lot of that—touching me instead of talking—and I was used to his silences now.

We reached the marker by the tree, stopping to pay our respects, tears in both our eyes as we grappled with the enormity of what had happened. He'd been shot in the throat and heart—died instantly or so they reassured us. He wouldn't have felt pain, and the remains we'd seen weren't him, because I truly believed, as did Kyle, that he was now part of nature.

When we reached the cabin, we sat on the small wall next to the door, right where everything had happened. Inside the cabin, it was just as it had been. Wilber's grandson was moving up from town to take his grandfather's place as unofficial caretaker of the woods, and it would be nice to have a new neighbor.

If I stayed here.

"We should probably talk," Kyle said and took my hand again, examining my palm as if he was searching for my lifeline. He traced each finger.

My stomach fell. This was the moment he explained that he was ready to go back to Boston, and then it was my turn to make my decision on what had to be the easiest and hardest question of all time. Hard because I would be turning my back on all of this, and easy because I would be with Kyle.

"Some people are born to play hockey, y'know?"

"Like you," I said with a smile.

"No, not like me," he said, and I cast a glance at his serious expression. "People like Tennant Rowe, Tate Collins, the phenoms, then goalies like Stan, men who talk to their posts, who love what they do, or the Arizona goalie who is just as mad and out there. These are the guys who carry teams, who are flash and excitement and you watch them and you can't help but be dazzled."

"I think that's you."

"I know I'm good at my job, or at least I was good—"

"You still can be. You are," I defended fiercely.

"I don't have the heart for it as they do. I don't want it with a hunger that burns, and I don't have the same passion I had that took me away from here, just so I could outrun my fears."

"Kyle—"

"No. Listen. I could play for a few more years, save the money, but I don't need it—I already have everything I want, and my contract was generous, so I have enough put away already, so I don't have to worry. You see money is a consideration and career fulfillment and all that."

I wasn't sure where this was going, but I got the feeling it was because he was having an internal debate and only verbalizing small pieces of what he was thinking. Everything sounded so disjointed, and then he stopped and gripped my hand. Now it was my turn to talk.

"I'll come to Boston with you," I blurted. I wasn't going to be the reason that he gave up his career. I could be the one to make the sacrifices needed to make sure we were never apart again because I loved him more than my next breath, and I wasn't losing him again.

"Huh?" He shifted on the wall and turned to stare at me, and he had the most confused expression I'd ever seen on him.

"I already talked to some people about retraining for the FEMA Urban Search and Rescue Task Force. It's in Beverly, which is only a short drive from Boston, and I could make that work if they wanted me."

"They'd be stupid not to want you," he said with a smile.

"Yeah." I sat back as if the decision was made. Now I just needed to break it to my mom and dad.

"They'll want you, but, Christian, they can't have you."

That put my back up. If he expected me to sit around with my thumb up my ass, he was wrong. "I have to do something. I can't sit around while you're off playing hockey, waiting for you to—"

"You're not listening to me," he interrupted with a hand on my chest. Then he frowned. "Or maybe I'm not explaining right. Christian, listen to me, okay. I'm staying here. I'm retiring. I'm going to spend time with you, with family. I'm going to help you build the garage shelter for the worst blizzards. I'm going to cover the store for you when you're off being heroic. I'll coach the Eagle Ridge Eaglets with you, maybe set up a summer camp for goalie prospects, invest in the rink here with you? I have a ton of wild ideas."

I stared at him, and I know my mouth was open because he used his index finger under my chin to shut it for me.

"Here?" I managed and then was struck dumb when he nodded.

"Christian. Talk to me… do you still want me here? Is there a place for me with you?"

"You're… you… here… with me…"

"Use your words, babe," he teased.

But I didn't talk—I kissed him with ruthless determination. Damn right there was a place for him here. With me.

I was *never* letting him go.

Epilogue

LIFE WAS SURREAL AND THAT WAS *NOT* BECAUSE I WAS seated next to a wizard and across from a druid. Although that did add to the overall oddness of the day.

"… entering the cave, you hear a sound. A sort of keening that sounds as if it might be a wild animal," Austin said, his brand-new *DUNGEON MASTER* T-shirt hidden behind his dungeon master screen.

"Do I know what it is?" Moral asked, his beard littered with muffin crumbs, as usual.

"Make an investigation check to see if your druid senses are familiar with the keening cry," Austin replied. I glanced over at Christian, who was smiling at how into the session most of my teammates were. I'd never been huge into the game, but since it was a team thing, I'd played along. Now that I was no longer a Rebel, it felt funny being included. Xander had assured me that this final session before my boyfriend and I drove the rented U-Haul truck back to Manitoba was a goodbye of sorts. A way to heroically end my character's arc, as I'd not be playing anymore.

Perhaps surreal wasn't the best way to describe my feelings. Bittersweet probably worked better. Maybe it was both.

Moral used his hand to fluff his beard. Crumbs flew to the table. Marquis gave him a dark look, then dusted off the papers, dice trays, and manuals that covered every inch of the tabletop. With a huff and a wink at me, Moral rolled his die.

"Fuck. Natural one." The big ginger sighed, then grabbed another raspberry muffin.

"You have no idea what that sound was." Austin, the new sole owner of the condo I used to own, gave the players an expectant look. "What do you want to do now?"

"How long does this last?" Christian whispered in my ear. We sat back to allow Robbie to place fresh cups of Bean Town Brew coffees and teas in front of us before he took his seat beside Austin. He'd be moving into my old place. They seemed incredibly happy.

"Oh, anywhere from an hour to five hours," I replied after thanking Robbie and passing a cup of Earl Grey decaf to Xander. He and Mason, his partner, were on this tea kick. They were making a lengthy trip to the UK over the summer—a trip they'd put on hold when they found out I was making one final visit to Boston to sign the sale papers and pack up what remained of my belongings—just so Xander could engage in one last session. It was so

Xander. Our captain was one of the best leaders I'd ever had the privilege of playing with. I'd miss him. Heck, I'd miss all of them, but my life was further north now. With Christian and my parents and the people of Eagle Ridge. We all had healing to do.

"Yikes," Christian softly replied, lifting the lid from his coffee. "Would anyone be mad if I did some reading while you played?"

"Nope." I smiled, then gave his knee a squeeze. He was taking a new helicopter safety training course that was being sponsored by the Search and Rescue Volunteer Association of Manitoba. It would up his certification level, while adding to his skills as a SAR Tech.

"So, what are you going to do up there with the polar bears?" Marquis enquired after taking his turn and using some sort of wizard spell to make tiny orbs float over our heads as we moved deeper into the cave.

"Heal," I softly replied. They all got sad looks, so I hurried to say something more uplifting. "Maybe coach some youth hockey. Help out at the store while my bf here becomes the most amazing SAR Tech in the province." Christian waved off the applause that broke out at our table. "What about you all?"

"I'm heading to Toronto for a few weeks. Robbie has some vacation time. Then, we're coming back here to work on our new place." Austin beamed at his man, who beamed right back. "Thanks again for giving me dibs on the condo, Kyle."

"You and Robbie just be happy there, okay?" I rapped

knuckles with the youngest Rowe. Then, my sight went to Xander. "I know you and Mason are doing this grand tour of England, Ireland, and Scotland."

"Yep," our captain said, popping his P as his eyes glowed with adoration. "I cannot wait. He's been working insane hours at the agency and is this close to a total burnout." He pinched some air with his fingers. "A month away sipping tea, eating haggis, and kissing Blarney Stones will be just what the doctor ordered. For both of us."

I nodded. It had been a rough season. Losing to the Railers had cut deep. And, then, my nightmare tale had made things topsy-turvy for the team for months. No wonder everyone wanted to get away from Boston.

"Moral, you have any plans?" I asked after rolling for initiative after Xander had stumbled across a dire wolf den filled with rabid canines with a taste for adventurers.

"Shit! Why are all my initiative roles for fucking bad? Fuck you, blue dice!" He tossed a blue die across the store, apologized to the dude whose coffee it splashed into, and then tugged on his beard in a shamefaced way. "I'm heading back to Canada for some R&R, maybe do some fishing and kayaking."

"They make kayaks big enough for you?" Marquis tossed out. Moral laughed loudly while patting his belly. It wasn't a pouchy gut at all. It was all muscle. *Lots* of muscle.

"And you, Marquis? What are you doing this summer?" I tossed my die and got a measly seven. Guess

I'd be last in the battle order. Which was fine. I wasn't much of a fighter, but I could viciously mock the hell out of enemies. Could you mock a wolf? I'd have to ask Austin.

"I'm stuck doing more international travel for my family company. My father and uncle are trying to lock up this deal to supply all the plumbing going into some new castle some rich prince in some snowy ass European country is refitting." He rolled brown eyes. "Not that I object to flying, or traveling, but I'd much rather be spending my downtime on a nude beach in Monaco, than courting some dusty old monarch in some dinky backwoods hamlet."

"First world problems," Joachim slid in as he sat down. Marquis flipped him off. "Sorry I'm late. Sophia was trying to climb from the couch to the coffee table and fell off. She's fine," he was quick to say when everyone gasped. "Just bumped her head. Isaac and I both had to fuss over her. Every time we turn our backs, she's climbing up something. This fatherhood stuff is taxing."

"You love every minute of it," Xander commented, and Joachim nodded. It was obvious to anyone who saw him that Joachim adored his daughter and Isaac. Happiness radiated out of him. Peeking over at Christian with his nose in his phone studying madly, I wondered if someday he and I could have that kind of home and kid life. Not the pro hockey aspect, obviously, as I'd left that in my past. It still hurt. Watching a dream die was never easy, but I needed peace. As I'd told the guys, I wanted nothing more than to heal and be whole. And the only way to be whole was to be with my other half. I felt Christian's gaze on me.

"Are you okay?" he asked in a whisper.

I nodded. I was very much okay. Maybe not great yet, but I was as happy as I'd been in forever. And that was all due in a monumentally large part to the man seated beside me. He'd saved me from being snowed under mentally, physically, and emotionally. He was the love of my life and now, finally, it was a life free from terrors.

"I've never been better."

THE END

What's next for the Rebels?

Royal Lines (Boston Rebels 4)

They're setting fire to the sheets, but a romance between an out and proud hockey star and a closeted playboy prince could end up burning them both.

Marquis Miller is a man known for living the high life. He might be one of the NHL's best-dressed players, single, wealthy, and open about his sexuality, but he knows his future lies in taking over the reins of the family's multimillion-dollar company after retirement. Jumping on the family jet, he heads to Europe, tasked with schmoozing a prince into accepting his company's bid on a significant castle renovation. Assuming he'd be faced with a dusty old monarch well into his dotage, Marquis is stunned to find out that Kaleb is a young, sophisticated, beautiful man with an impressive work ethic, to-die-for eyes, and a certain flair that captures Marquis's attention.

Dragging the royal palace into the twenty-first century is one battle after another for the King's youngest son. Juggling renovations, his royal duties, and attempting to reverse his former playboy prince reputation is impossible when no one seems to want to give Kaleb a chance. His chaotic life takes yet another turn when an American hockey player arrives at the castle to discuss a renovation project. Marquis is the antithesis of Kaleb's newly minted, responsible outlook on life, a jock, a player, willing to take chances. Although the forbidden sex is hot, Kaleb is not ready to turn on his family responsibilities for a pretty smile and a smart mouth.

For both men, family is everything, and romance will always come in second until they open their hearts to love.

Hockey Series' from RJ Scott & V.L. Locey

Harrisburg Railers

Owatonna U Hockey

Arizona Raptors

Boston Rebels

LA Storm

Chesterford Coyotes - Young Adult

Free Reads

Please note - in all of these free stories, there will be some spoilers for the main series books.

Railers Short Stories

Volume 1 | Volume 2

LA Storm

Sparkle

The Colts - AHL Short Stories

Pucks & Percentages

Breakaway

Making the Save

Standalone

Waiting for Christmas

Harrisburg Railers

When hockey wunderkind Tennant Rowe meets his new coach, he knows he's in trouble. Jared Madsen is nine years older than Tennant, impossibly attractive, and — worst of all — his brother's off-limits best friend. Is their chemistry worth the risk?

Changing Lines (Railers 1)

Can Tennant show Jared that age is just a number, and that love is all that matters?

The Rowe Brothers are famous hockey hotshots, but as the youngest of the trio, Tennant has always had to play against his brothers' reputations. To get out of their shadows, and against their advice, he accepts a trade to the Harrisburg Railers, where he runs into Jared Madsen. Mads is an old family friend and his brother's one-time teammate. Mads is Tennant's new coach. And Mads is the sexiest thing he's ever laid eyes on.

Jared Madsen's hockey career was cut short by a fault in his heart, but coaching keeps him close to the game. When Ten is traded to the team, his carefully organized world is thrown into chaos. Nine years his junior and his best friend's brother, he knows Ten is strictly off-limits, but as soon as he sees Ten's moves, on and off the ice, he knows that his heart could get him into trouble again.

Changing Lines

Harrisburg Railers (Hockey Romance)

1. Changing Lines
2. First Season
3. Deep Edge
4. Poke Check
5. Last Defense
6. Goal Line
7. Neutral Zone
8. Hat Trick
9. Save The Date
10. Baby Makes Three
11. Rivals
12. Perfect Gifts
13. Family First

Meet the men of Owatonna University's hockey team

Ryker (Owatonna U, 1)

Ryker

Ryker is hockey royalty, Jacob is a poor country boy. Can two vastly different people find common ground and become the men they want to be?

Ryker comes from a long line of championship-winning hockey players. Playing college hockey to develop his game is his only focus, and nothing will stand in the way of him working to become the best player. He has no room for relationships, people who point out his flaws, or anyone who calls him on his dreams. He certainly has no place for love, and meeting Jacob is nothing but a useful distraction on the side. After all trying to get his Owatonna Eagles teammate into bed is less work and more play. When tragedy rocks his family, his charmed life crumbles, and the only person he can turn to is the same one who claims to hate him.

Jacob Benson has only known hard work and stifling conservative values his whole life. Born and raised in the small rural community of Eden Crossing, Minnesota, he's the only son of a hard-working but struggling dairy farming family. Jacob is using his skills in hockey to finance his way to an agricultural science degree. These four years at Owatonna U. will probably be the only time he has to enjoy life, gain acceptance about his sexuality, and live openly before his inevitable return to the farm. Running into a pretty rich boy like Ryker Madsen is putting a damper on his enjoyment of life away from home. Ryker's flip, conceited, carefree attitude grates on Jacob's every nerve. So why, if Ryker is everything he dislikes, does he want nothing more than to explore the sinful dreams that his annoying teammate stars in every night?

Ryker

––––––––

Owatonna U Hockey (Hockey Romance)

1. Ryker

Coast to Coast (Arizona Raptors 1)

Coast To Coast

When opposites attract, this bottom-of-the-league team will never be the same again.

A stipulation in his father's will forces Mark back into the arms of a family that disowned him and leaves him one-third owner of a hockey team facing financial ruin. He doesn't even watch hockey, let alone like it, and wants nothing more than to head back to New York. Then there's the new coach, a stubborn, opinionated, irritating man with superiority issues and questionable music taste. Butting heads with Rowen becomes the new normal, but it comes with passionate debate and an all-consuming lust.

Challenged to rebuild one of the worst teams in the league into a future cup contender, Rowen can't pass up the opportunity. Never in his twenty years of hockey has he ever seen a team managed so badly or coached players overflowing with resentment and bigotry. Yet there's something about this team and this city that compels him to roll up his sleeves and start dismantling. If only Mark, one of three siblings who now own the Raptors, wasn't so damned rock-headed yet so damned appealing his job might be easier. It doesn't look like either is willing to give in, but one night in a dark, desert hotel changes everything.

Coast To Coast

Arizona Raptors (Hockey Romance)

1. Coast To Coast
2. Across the Pond
3. Shadow and Light
4. Sugar and Ice
5. School and Rock

LA Storm

Script (LA Storm, 1)

Script

Hollywood A-lister Finn might be Canadian, but he needs Cameron to show him how to hockey.

Actor Finn Kerrigan is at a crossroads. After growing up a soap star, then starring in a hugely successful trilogy of action movies, he's finally given the chance to read a heartfelt and passionate script that could change his life forever. The role would be enough for people to see him as a serious actor, and maybe even win him an award or two (and no, a golden raspberry award for his action movies doesn't count). Once established as a serious actor he's sure he can come out of the closet and finally live his truth. When he lies to get the part of a hockey player on a struggling team, he suddenly has nowhere to hide. He might be Canadian, but the last time he skated he was ten, and no, he doesn't have hockey in his blood. With only a month until filming starts, he about to be exposed, but partnered with a player who's supposed to be giving him tips, he doesn't realize how many of his secrets will come to light. Falling in lust, one heated kiss at a time, is inevitable, but giving Cameron up at the end of the shoot could break his heart.

Cameron Chavkin is the face of the LA Storm. And the body, and the hair, and the smile. He's at the prime of his career, men and women want to be with him, and he's skating better than he ever has before. His house sits next to a famous rock star's mansion, his garage is filled with expensive cars, and he's even been asked to mentor a once-famous actor in a new hockey movie. Life is pretty sweet. Until the bad boy of hockey meets Finn, a man on the edge with more secrets than Cameron has endorsements. Knowing better than to get involved, Cameron is swept up despite himself, and when it's time to say goodbye to the Storm's most eligible bachelor is finding it hard to follow the script.

Script

LA Storm

1. Script

2. Second
3. Shield
4. Spiral

Off The Ice (Chesterford Coyotes, 1)

Off The Ice

A coming-of-age love story with high school, hockey rivalry, friendship, family, and coming out.

Soren's life changes in an instant when he and his younger brother are adopted by hockey royalty. Making sense of his new life is hard enough, but when he's enrolled in a private school it means facing a whole new set of problems. Navigating friendship, family, and hockey is one thing, but being attracted to the boy who vexes him is a whole new thing.

Felix has a reputation to protect. He's the kid who seems to have everything but looks can be deceiving. Spinning lies about his perfect life, he's created a fantasy world that even he has started to believe. Only, it's not long before everything crumbles, all of his pretty lies are revealed, and only his closest rival sees through his pain and stands by him.

Fighting is easy, friendship is hard, but love is everything.

Off The Ice

Chesterford Coyotes

1. Off The Ice
2. On Thin Ice
3. *Dance on Ice*

Also By RJ Scott

For a full list of ebooks and links please scan the code above or
visit rjscott.co.uk/rjbooks

Meet RJ Scott

RJ discovered romance in books at a very young age and realized that if there wasn't romance on the page, she could create it in her head. With over one hundred and fifty books published, she is a full time author of gay romance.

She lives and works out of her home in the beautiful English countryside, spends her spare time reading, watching films, and enjoying time with her family.

The last time she had a week's break from writing she didn't like it one little bit and has yet to meet a box of chocolates she couldn't defeat.

www.rjscott.co.uk | rj@rjscott.co.uk

NEWSLETTER - rjscott.co.uk/rjnews

facebook.com/author.rjscott

x.com/Rjscott_author

instagram.com/rjscott_author

amazon.com/author/rj-scott

bookbub.com/authors/rj-scott

goodreads.com/rjscott

pinterest.com/rjscottauthor

Also By VL Locey

For a full list of ebooks and links please scan the code above or visit vllocey.com/stories-from-vl-locey

Meet V.L. Locey

V.L. Locey loves worn jeans, yoga, belly laughs, walking, reading and writing lusty tales, Greek mythology, the New York Rangers, comic books, and coffee.

(Not necessarily in that order.)

She shares her life with her husband, her daughter, one dog, two cats, a flock of assorted domestic fowl, and two Jersey steers.

When not writing spicy romances, she enjoys spending her day with her menagerie in the rolling hills of Pennsylvania with a cup of fresh java in hand.

vllocey.com

vicki@vllocey.com

Newsletter - vllocey.com/newsletter

facebook.com/V.L.Locey

x.com/vllocey

instagram.com/vl_locey

bookbub.com/authors/v-l-locey

goodreads.com/vllocey

pinterest.com/vllocey

www.ingramcontent.com/pod-product-compliance
Lightning Source LLC
Chambersburg PA
CBHW060915250626
47159CB00008B/3021

* 9 7 8 1 7 8 5 6 4 5 8 8 4 *